TWO IF BY SEA

PETER J. LEVESQUE

MINDSTIR MEDIA

Two If By Sea

Published by Mindstir Media, LLC
45 Lafayette Rd | Suite 181| North Hampton, NH 03862 | USA
1.800.767.0531 | www.mindstirmedia.com

Printed in the United States of America
ISBN: 979-8-9863201-8-2 (paperback)
ISBN: 979-8-9863201-9-9 (hardback)

To Lisa, Catherine, Paul and Matthew, and
for my parents, Paul and Mary Levesque

"There is nothing more difficult to take in hand,
more perilous to conduct, or more uncertain in its success,
than to take the lead in the introduction
of a new order of things."

Machiavelli

PROLOGUE

Milton, Massachusetts: June 1, 2003

A bright afternoon sun beamed down on Milton Academy as the Class of 2003 graduation ceremony drew to a close. Parents and grandparents waded frantically between metal folding chairs, scrambling to organize family photographs. Through the commotion, two of Milton's top students found a quiet moment under a sprawling oak to reflect on their boarding school experience and say their goodbyes.

They had begun their time at Milton as total strangers but quickly became the best of friends. Along with a love of American history, they enjoyed competitive sports, beer pong, and dating coeds. The two young men shook hands under the tree and promised to stay in touch. Both were heading to top military schools, and each had a deeply personal reason for wanting to serve their country. James Francis Keenan was off to the United States Naval Academy. His roommate, Jiang Peng, was heading home to Beijing, to attend the People's Liberation Army National Defense School.

As the elated graduates and their exhausted families departed the day's ceremonies, they strolled beneath the school's stone archway inscribed with the Academy's motto: *Dare to Be True.* The motto dated back to 1898. No one could have imagined that the survival of the free world would someday depend on it.

THE ORGAN DONOR PROGRAM

CHAPTER 1

Tilanqiao Prison, Shanghai China

Every square inch of Shanghai's notorious Tilanqiao Prison reeked of human waste and body odor. The compound's dingy façade and decrepit interior had remained untouched since its construction by British and American troops more than a century before. China's Ministry of State Security considered Tilanqiao its showpiece for political incarceration and torture. No one had ever escaped from Tilanqiao, and few had tried. Inmates called it the Alcatraz of the Orient.

Prisoner 6468 sat in his cell, dressed in dingy orange overalls, grey socks, and black slippers. Not allowed to wash or shave for over a week, he had a pale and clammy complexion, his prison overalls stained with perspiration.

Military guards wearing their green dress uniforms and bright white gloves entered his cell, quickly applying handcuffs and leg shackles. The prisoner's nervous heart began to race as he walked down the dimly lit hallway and out into the large rectangular prison yard. It had been three weeks since he had last seen daylight, and his eyes blinked uncontrollably in the bright afternoon sun.

More than three hundred inmates were paraded around the yard's perimeter, their overalls painting a swath of bright orange against the yard's filthy grey walls. As they looked on in silence, the condemned prisoner was shuffled into the center of the courtyard, ankle chains rattling. The guards held his elbows and shoulders tightly, forcing him to stand at attention in front of the prison's infamous Warden Tan.

The Warden opened a small brown envelope containing the official sentencing decree from Beijing's High Court and read it aloud:

"Prisoner 6468 has been found guilty of high treason by the People's Republic of China and is hereby sentenced to death. By order of the High Court, the sentence is to be carried out immediately."

The inmate struggled to hear the Warden's proclamation while half dazed, his legs wobbly and giving way beneath him as the gruesome process of the execution began. He was forced to kneel on the yard's cobblestones, pain shooting into his knees. A dirty washcloth from the prison's canteen was tied around the prisoner's head, serving as a makeshift blindfold. It reeked of garbage, just as the Warden had intended.

No last words are granted for the crime of treason. Kneeling on the rough stones beneath his knees, the prisoner agonized over when the bullet would come. Would it be painful? Would he be aware of the lethal projectile shooting through his brain? He tried to picture his wife's face, determined to be in control of his final thoughts, but fear overtook him, and he helplessly urinated.

For the more seasoned inmates at Tilanqiao, public executions were nothing new. Among the rookies, however, extreme agitation and nervous fidgeting occurred in the ranks. They looked on in silence as a tall executioner from Shanghai's army garrison walked over and stood behind the kneeling prisoner.

Drawing his QSZ-92 service revolver, the experienced soldier aimed his pistol just inches from the back of the skull. A loud crack rang across the courtyard as the bullet fired into the prisoner's head, exiting just above the nose, as the body tumbled awkwardly to the ground. A pool of blood grew rapidly around what remained of the inmate's head. The prison rookies gagged and vomited where they stood.

Six inmates chosen from the gallery carried the body to the infirmary. They were given plastic trash bags to cover what remained of the prisoner's head and collect the brain matter and skull fragments scattered in the courtyard.

Warden Tan took a deep breath of satisfaction as he bent down to collect the spent bullet casing nestled between two odd-shaped cobblestone bricks. He placed the casing in an envelope along with an invoice for Twenty-three Yuan, the cost of the executioner's bullet, which he handed to his deputy. "I want you to personally deliver this to the traitor's wife," the Warden instructed. "And wait there until she pays the bill in full."

From the prison's infirmary, a doctor from Shanghai University Hospital began the task of harvesting the prisoner's liver, kidneys, and heart. The organs had been carefully screened in advance of the execution and were cross-matched to a list of Chinese officials anxiously awaiting a donor. Organ donations through the national prison system were a valuable perk for Beijing's elite and their families. China's prisoners were less enthusiastic about the program.

The headless and harvested remains of 6468 were shoveled into a body bag and thrown into the prison's furnace, sending a familiar stench up the chimney and into the surrounding neighborhood as a pungent reminder to anyone with unpatriotic thoughts. The dead prisoner was now just a small pile of ashes, forgotten and inconsequential. Or so China thought.

PILGRIM

CHAPTER 2

CIA Headquarters, Langley Virginia

On Thursday afternoon inside CIA headquarters, James Francis Keenan sat at his desk fidgeting with an empty coffee mug, anticipating an urgent phone call from Beijing. At thirty-four, he was the youngest agent to ever run the Agency's coveted China desk. Women found him irresistible at just over six feet tall with a strong athletic build, steel blue eyes, and a handsome face. His analytical mind, managerial expertise, and seasoned language skills were what made him most attractive to the CIA.

Keenan stared out his office window at the green foliage outside. Though invisible to the naked eye, the glass at Langley vibrated at a very low frequency to deflect foreign listening devices aimed at the building. Jim found the Agency's technology fascinating. *Our people think of everything*, he thought.

The phone rang at exactly 1400 hours, as scheduled.

"Sir, I have Beijing on security line two," Keenan's assistant announced through the intercom.

"Put it through, please, Angela."

China was twelve hours ahead of Langley, and the call was from Agent Ken Barrow, the CIA's Chief of Station at the U.S. Embassy in Beijing.

"Hello, Ken." Keenan's tone was somber.

"Good afternoon, Jim. Wish I had better news for you. We can confirm that Pilgrim was executed at Tilanqiao Prison yesterday. Shot in the head."

Keenan squeezed the phone receiver. Slumping forward in his chair, he rested his elbows on his desk as he held the phone with his left hand and rubbed his forehead with his right.

Wen Bao, code name Pilgrim, was the CIA's twelfth asset in China to be executed over the last six months. As Keenan listened to the rest of Barrow's report from Beijing, he came to terms with what he had long suspected.

"I can't believe we have a fucking mole, Ken!" Keenan exclaimed.

"Looks that way. We'll start our internal sweep over here, Jim. Do let us know what the next move is when you can."

The call abruptly ended. Keenan silently contemplated the magnitude of the challenge that lay ahead. Of the twenty assets he was currently running in China, more than half were now confirmed dead. There was only one way that could happen. Someone inside his top-secret operation was giving names to the Ministry of State Security in Beijing.

Saving his remaining operatives in China would be next to impossible without leads or evidence.

He had a difficult phone call to make. This time to his boss.

Jim pressed the intercom. "Angela, get Tom Fahey on the line, please."

He looked up at the digital clock on his office wall, it was 14:25. He had already been in the office for thirteen hours. *It's going to be a long fucking day.*

Angela's voice came over the intercom: "I've got Director of Operations, Tom Fahey on line one."

★★★

At fifty-six, Tom Fahey was a spy right out of central casting. Born in Goa, India, to American diplomats, he was tall and slim with salt-and-pepper hair, dark brown eyes, and a photographic memory. With his warm and fatherly personality, he spoke in low tones that put everyone around him at ease. His signature wardrobe of fitted black suits, red pocket square handkerchiefs, and polished black shoes was legendary. He oozed intelligence and quiet sophistication.

Fahey was a legacy at CIA, his father having served as the Agency's Chief of Station in India before being killed on special assignment in Saigon, a sacrifice denoted by a nameless black peg on the memorial wall at Langley. Like his father, Fahey attended Williams College and then London School of Economics where he studied journalism and communications. Writing was his true passion, and he treasured his time as a war correspondent for the *New York Times*. While covering the Rwanda genocide story in 1994, he decided that finding solutions to global conflicts would be a more meaningful career than just writing about them. Entering the family spy business seemed pre-ordained, and he was accepted into the CIA fraternity with great enthusiasm. His career skyrocketed with stints in Panama, Istanbul, Iran, and five years in Beijing where he became fluent in Mandarin.

The deep relationships that Fahey was able to cultivate with the leadership in Beijing catapulted his career at the Agency. Using his Commercial Service cover to connect foreign investors with Chinese development projects, he was able to penetrate and befriend Beijing's highest levels of government. With the Agency's permission, he married May Chiu, the well-educated and socially prominent daughter of a PLA Army general, enhancing his status in Beijing. Mainland China was on the precipice of the greatest economic miracle of the 20th century, and Fahey found himself at the center of it, rubbing shoulders with China's elites while providing a treasure trove of intelligence back to Langley. His promotion to CIA Director of Operations was a forgone conclusion.

"I agree with your assessment, Jim. Has to be a mole," Fahey said calmly. "I'll brief Director Wentworth. Stand by for a trip to the White House."

Keenan ended the call and quietly awaited further instructions.

THE MAN WITH THE LITTLE HEAD

CHAPTER 3

Office of the Director of Central Intelligence, Langley Virginia

Charles Wentworth III sat behind a large mahogany desk that seemed to overwhelm his diminutive body. The Director of the CIA resembled a child needing a booster seat. His office was tastefully appointed with deep brown mahogany walls and matching mahogany bookcases that were accented with blue and white China porcelain vases. He liked to describe the décor as government-issued elegance.

At sixty-two years old, the Director looked more like eighty. He was the second Director of Central Intelligence in just three years, his predecessor having resigned for personal reasons involving a penchant for five-star hotels with high-end prostitutes. Wentworth was one of only a handful of nominees confirmed by the Senate in a presidential administration plagued by controversy and government vacancies. At five feet six inches tall with a slender physique, pale complexion, wire-rimmed glasses, and an unusually small head, Wentworth commanded no physical presence whatsoever. Wearing a wrinkled blue suit with a wrinkled white button-down shirt, brown shoes, and a red tie, he could have been mistaken for a stockbroker who had been out all night, entertaining clients.

Wentworth had reportedly made a fortune in the energy fracking business in West Texas. His only hobbies were drinking copious amounts of scotch, high-stakes poker games, and horse racing. His demeanor was secretive, nervous, and somewhat paranoid. His business dealings were always ambiguous if not outright mysterious, a fact the Senate chose to ignore during his confirmation hearings. The only spy experience Wentworth had was the private detective he had once hired to catch his cheating wife. That spy mission was a success. His marriage was not.

What no one inside the Beltway questioned was Charles Wentworth's ability to raise hundreds of millions of dollars for the Republican National Committee. In a town run by money and more money, Wentworth's funding of Republican incumbents was the only qualification he needed to be confirmed as Director of the Central Intelligence Agency.

"Sir, Tom Fahey is here for your meeting," his assistant William Barger announced at the door.

"Good morning, Sir," Tom smiled as he stepped into the room.

"Please have a seat, Tom," the Director gestured.

They shook hands, and Fahey sat down in one of the leather chairs facing the Director's desk. He had tutored numerous freshman CIA Directors over the years, helping them get the lay of the land and catch up on intelligence operations. From Fahey's perspective, there was always political capital to be gained in teaching the boss how things worked.

He found himself trying not to focus on Wentworth's unusually small head, which barely cleared the height of his desk. He had done his own research on the new boss as any good company man would do. Most of Wentworth's history checked out, including several prior divorces, but there were unexplained gaps when it came to his net worth and exactly how he had made his money. He had done several questionable deals with China over the years. His tax returns from the last decade were all under IRS audit, and it was impossible to determine how much money the Director had or how much he owed. Although required by law, there was no indication that Wentworth had established a blind trust for his stock portfolio. Fahey could only accept the perceived legitimacy of his current boss and serve him the best he could until the next Director came along.

Fahey stood from his seat and handed Wentworth a large green personnel file. The name on the file was James Francis Keenan.

"Well, Tom," the little head began to speak, "they say good news takes the stairs, and bad news takes the elevator."

"Sir?" Fahey queried, resuming his seat.

"I hear we've got a mole inside the CIA. Ambassador Bowlen in Beijing is an old friend of mine. He gave me a ring last night and filled me in."

"Yes, Sir," Fahey replied, somewhat agitated with the loose-lipped Ambassador in China. "It does appear we have a mole, Sir. And I brought James Keenan's file to review, as you requested."

The slight figure opened the file and pretended to read for a moment. "So, tell me what we know about Mr. Keenan," Wentworth requested.

"Well, Sir," Fahey began, "Jim is an American success story. He's one of those kids from the 9-11 era on a quest to make a difference in the world."

"What do you mean?"

"Keenan is thirty-four, born in Brookline, Massachusetts. His father David Keenan was an executive at State Street Bank in Boston. His mother Mary trained as a registered nurse. In 1988 when Jim was three years old, his father took a foreign assignment in Hong Kong running the bank's Asia Pacific division. The family moved to Asia, and Jim attended the Hong Kong American School where he learned Mandarin Chinese."

"Amazing how kids can absorb languages," the smallish head chimed in.

"Yes, Sir," Fahey continued politely. "The family moved back to Brookline in August 2001 when Jim was sixteen. He was accepted at Milton Academy Boarding School in Massachusetts."

"Milton!" Wentworth exclaimed. "My son went to Milton. *Dare to be True*. Great school."

"Yes," Fahey continued. "Keenan's roommate at Milton was Jiang Peng, the son of China's current President Jiang. According to the school's Headmaster, the two boys were inseparable. They even started a U.S. History Club at Milton that continues to this day."

"Is Keenan still in contact with Jiang?"

"We're not sure, Sir. They had a falling out a couple of years ago. Keenan doesn't talk about it, but it appears to have been a difference of opinion over Beijing's motives in Hong Kong. They also have their respective security clearances to consider when it comes to staying in touch."

"Were these guys queers at Milton?" the little head inquired.

"There is no indication of that, Sir, and given Keenan's popularity and track record with women, it seems unlikely."

"What does that mean?" Wentworth asked.

"I'll get to that in a minute, Sir." Fahey cleared his throat before continuing. "According to his psychological profile, Keenan experienced two traumatic events when he was an early teen. You might recall the story in the media years ago about the Hong Kong American School sex scandal?"

"The pedophile fiasco? Keenan was abused?"

"Not exactly. The school's Principal ran a sophisticated pedophile ring together with the high school's guidance counselor. They were like Jeffrey Epstein and that Maxwell woman, using Hong Kong as their fantasy island."

Wentworth nodded in recollection of the news report.

Fahey resumed. "Anyway, the pair developed an enormous clientele of male customers looking for young boys, with some wealthy clients flying in from as far away as Bangkok."

"Clients leaving the sex-crazed capital of Bangkok to have more sex in Hong Kong?" Wentworth chuckled at the irony and shook his head in disgust.

"They ran the entire operation out of the Principal's apartment, literally under the noses of the parents where many of the children lived. They also took their little show on the road, taking advantage of the school's field trips around Asia to broaden their customer base."

"That's sick."

"At the trial, the Principal testified that the Head of School caught on to the sex ring early on. But instead of alerting the authorities, he became the ring's biggest customer. He never actually paid for the sex services. It was sort of 'professional courtesy' among school administrators is the way the Principal described it in his testimony."

"That's really twisted," said the little head, shrinking into his seat.

"It gets worse. Keenan's best friend at the time was one of the sex ring's victims. The kid was too embarrassed to tell his parents. One day he just hurled himself in front of a speeding MTR subway train. The kid had written a note describing what was happening over at the Principal's apartment. That broke the story wide open. Keenan was completely devastated at the loss of his close friend."

"Unbelievable."

"Keenan was called to testify in court. He said that the school's administrators all enjoyed what he called *emotional pedophilia*."

"Emotional pedophilia?" Wentworth's eyebrows rose.

"Yes. Keenan testified that school administrators got off on fucking with kids' heads," Fahey said somberly. "The three administrators who were convicted received life sentences at Stanley Prison. What they didn't know was that the son of Hong Kong's most notorious Triad gang leaders had been one of their victims. Their life sentences lasted only about two months once the Triad gangs got hold of them in prison."

"Justice served, I suppose. I'm afraid to ask about the second traumatic event," Wentworth offered as he adjusted himself in his seat.

"It doesn't get much better, I'm afraid."

"Well then let's hear it."

"On September eleventh…"

"Oh no," Wentworth mumbled.

"Keenan's father boarded United flight 175 in Boston to attend a banking conference in Los Angeles. At 9:03 the plane slammed into the World Trade Center. Jim was watching the attack on television with his classmates in the Schwarz Student Center at Milton, unaware that his father was on that flight. Milton's headmaster called him up to his office. Jim's mother was on the phone and told him the tragic news."

Wentworth looked up at Fahey and shook his head in horror. "So, Keenan's motivation to serve his country is to avenge his father's death? A bit cliché, isn't it, Tom?" the small head asked. "Keenan says that to deal with the shock and grief of losing his father, he made a promise to himself that he would serve in the U.S. military and help prevent another attack from ever happening. You recall we had a major spike in military recruitment after the 9-11 attacks from young men and women across the country who wanted to do the same thing."

"Yes, I do recall."

"Keenan was accepted into the Naval Academy, Midshipman Class of 2007. Graduated first in his class and then off to flight school where he learned to fly the F-18 Hornet."

Scrolling through the file's documents, the little head chimed in. "Says here his Navy call sign was Camelot?"

"Yes, Sir. His flight squadron leader told us they gave him that call sign because he was from Boston, his initials were J.F.K., and because Jim's success with women seemed to mimic the late President's libido."

"That's the second time you've brought up Keenan's relations with women. Could you elaborate? That's an order, by the way."

"Well, Sir, women consider Keenan to be quite attractive. He dates around, but he is unable or unwilling to make a long-term commitment."

"What's wrong with that?" Wentworth chimed in. "I've had four marriages so far that were supposed to last a lifetime. My last wife slept with half of Fort Worth, Texas, before taking me to the cleaners."

"Keenan's psychological profile says that the suicide of his close friend in Hong Kong and the tragic loss of his father on 9-11 left him unable or unwilling to become emotionally attached to anyone for fear of losing them. Keenan says that his work is his top priority, and he doesn't have the time or interest in developing a meaningful relationship."

"Now we're getting somewhere. Please continue."

Tom reflected a moment. "The Navy encouraged Keenan to maintain his Mandarin language skills and paid him a monthly stipend to stay fluent, using a private tutor. When his flying days were over, he was a natural choice to join us here at the Agency. I recruited him myself, Sir."

"Anything in particular stand out while you were recruiting him?" Wentworth asked, looking shorter than ever as he slumped in his desk chair.

"His sense of humor," Fahey replied. "It's a key indication of high emotional intelligence."

"How so?" Wentworth's interest was heightened.

"It's been proven that people with a good sense of humor have better cognitive and emotional abilities. Higher verbal and non-verbal intelligence. Keenan is quick witted, a byproduct of his Irish roots, possibly. When I asked him what it was like to land an F-18 fighter jet on a pitching aircraft carrier deck, he jokingly told me it was like having sex during a car accident."

Wentworth looked up at Fahey, unimpressed, confirming he had no sense of humor. "I have just one question at this point, Tom. Would you stake your reputation on Jim Keenan given his longstanding relationship with the son of China's President and say that you're convinced he's not the mole we're looking for?"

"Yes, Sir, I would. I know this man. He is like a son to me. I should mention that as standard operating procedure, I ran Jim through all our counterintelligence protocols when we learned about the initial executions in China. Several hours of questioning and a polygraph test."

"And?"

"He passed with flying colors."

Wentworth slowly closed Keenan's file and looked up from his desk.

"Before we go to brief the President on the mole situation, tell me all I need to know about PROJECT LUCY."

THE BLAKELY DOCTRINE

CHAPTER 4

Office of the Director of Central Intelligence, Langley Virginia

"Should we take a nature break first?" Wentworth suggested, pushing his chair back and standing, which did not substantially improve his height. He and Fahey left the Director's office briefly and refilled their coffee mugs before sitting down again.

"How well do you know President Blakely?" Fahey asked the Director, resuming their meeting.

Wentworth leaned back. "We've known each other for many years. I first met him when I was hosting a fundraising event for George W. Bush in Dallas. Blakely was quite generous in donating to our political action committee. We found out later that he was equally generous in donating to the Gore campaign. The man hedges his bets."

"Not when it comes to China," Fahey interjected.

"What do you mean?" Wentworth queried.

"He's doubling down on Beijing to make sure we win the new Cold War."

Wentworth's eyes narrowed. "You really think we're in another Cold War?"

Nodding, Fahey replied, "I've been around China a long time, Sir. I was stationed there, as you know. Learned the language. Married a Chinese woman. Conducted business there. I think the Chinese also feel we're in a Cold War, and they're just as determined to win it. Payback for what they call their century of humiliation at the hands of the West."

Giving Fahey a speculative look, Wentworth replied, "Forgive me for saying so, Tom, but you seem to be a bit sympathetic to the Chinese."

"To be clear, Sir, I have a soft spot for the Chinese people, not for Beijing. I understand China's position. They are proud of their new status on the world stage. Proud they have lifted over 200 million people out of poverty over the last twenty years. I guess I just don't see any upside in pushing China to the brink of war."

"You mean an actual war?"

Tom weighed his words before speaking. "There are many examples throughout history of what happens when a rising power threatens to overtake an incumbent power. Tensions lead to all-out war, like when Athens challenged Sparta or Germany challenged Great Britain."

"Thucydides Trap," Wentworth said.

"Exactly," Fahey replied firmly, impressed that the Director had done his homework.

"I remember when Lyndon Johnson was so pissed off over the fact that another nation had achieved technological superiority over the United States," Wentworth went on. "And Johnson wasn't talking about China back then. He was talking about the Russians after their surprise launch of Sputnik. And if I recall correctly, Tom, we kicked Russia's ass in every way possible after that."

"Yes, Sir."

"And so, what exactly is your position on China, Tom?" Wentworth knit his fingers together on the desk in anticipation of the answer.

"Sir, I serve the Administration. My position is whatever the White House tells me it is."

"Off the record, Tom. Please. I would like to get your unfiltered opinion. It will help me to balance what's being discussed over at the White House."

Fahey paused. "Off the record, I believe we have a loose cannon on our hands with this President. Our goal at the Agency is to confront China and prevent World War III. This President makes snap decisions. He went against the advice of his intelligence and military advisors, to evacuate our troops from Afghanistan. That turned into a complete cluster fuck. Now we face a power vacuum in the Middle East that the Taliban and Al-Qaeda are exploiting to recruit a new generation of terrorists. The President is not an intellectual—he's a businessman—shrewd in profits, lost in policy. No offense, Sir."

"None taken." The little head bobbed agreeably.

"He processes complex issues by breaking them down into basic component parts, which leads him to define the world in simplistic terms: up and down, left and right, good and evil. And China fits squarely in the President's definition of evil."

"And you don't agree?"

Fahey sighed and leaned back. "China is a complicated culture that dates back thousands of years. It can't be reduced to a speaking note on an index card."

Wentworth considered this and gave Fahey a thoughtful glance. "Tom, the fact is, the Chinese are screwing us. They have been for years. They steal our intellectual property, they take our technology, and they block us from competing in their markets. This *businessman* President is the first leader to have the balls to say 'enough.' And that's what the Blakely Doctrine is all about. Contain and restrain China's rise by any means. Don't let China win on the backs of our ingenuity and elbow grease."

Fahey leaned forward. "I understand that, Sir. But there is nothing worse than an enemy with nothing to lose. If we push too hard, we risk backing China into a corner where they have no choice but to react. They move to invade Taiwan, for example. That will force a U.S. response that could lead us to the point of no return. A standoff that neither side is capable of backing away from."

"And PROJECT LUCY?" Wentworth asked to get the meeting back on track.

"Sir, PROJECT LUCY was put in place by Langley and the NSA as part of the Blakely Doctrine. Its objective is to head off Beijing's so called *Made in China 2025* scheme to dominate AI, robotics and aerospace technology over the next few years."

"But don't they need our semiconductor chips for that plan to be successful?" the Director asked.

"Yes. For all their advancements, China still has not been able to develop chip technology that can compete with the power and speed of American chip design. It's our secret sauce, and PROJECT LUCY was launched to make sure we keep our secret sauce away from their global ambitions. Our goal is to surveil China's technological development from the inside, determine how far they have come in microchip development, and use all means necessary to ensure they don't get any further. We have assets inside China's largest technology companies and research centers, and under Jim Keenan's leadership the program has been a major success."

"Until?"

"Until our assets started getting killed. Twelve executed over the last six months. The biggest hit to PROJECT LUCY came yesterday with the execution of Wen Bao, code name Pilgrim. He was an MIT-trained computer scientist working on the Sunway Supercomputer in Shanghai. We hear that computer can perform ninety-three trillion calculations per second. Pilgrim was providing us valuable intel on the computer's capabilities and the microchips used to power it. Now he's dead."

"So there has to be a mole. No other explanation."

"No other way to explain it, Sir. China's Ministry of State Security has the names of our assets."

Wentworth took a deep breath and exhaled slowly. "I'll schedule a briefing tomorrow with the President."

"Sir, Keenan and I have a meeting with the FBI counter-intelligence team tomorrow morning 08:00 at their request. They have some related developments to share with us. I suggest we brief the President after we learn what they have to say."

"I'd like to join you tomorrow, Tom, and also have FBI Director Susan Kendall join as well. This is big. We all need to be on the same page at the same time."

"Agreed, Sir."

Tom Fahey left Wentworth's office and headed back to his own. It was his first in-depth conversation with the new CIA Director, and he found himself surprisingly impressed by the inquisitive man with the little head.

REVELATIONS

CHAPTER 5

FBI Headquarters, Counterintelligence Division: Washington D.C.

Jim Keenan and Tom Fahey headed to the J. Edgar Hoover Building in a black Chevy suburban, which were ubiquitous on the streets of D.C.

"You seem anxious, Jim," Fahey inquired, noticing his friend was quieter than usual.

Jim stared out the window. "We're about to admit to the FBI that we have a mole at the CIA. That's just fucking embarrassing, Tom. And since the FBI called this meeting, they're probably going to tell us who the mole is, like we're incompetent boobs."

"This isn't your fault. We operate in an ambiguous environment, and we deal with a sordid cast of characters—shit happens. We need to mitigate the damage and move on."

"I'm responsible for those twelve dead assets, Tom, and if we don't identify the traitor soon, there will be even more dead people on my watch. How am I supposed to recruit assets in the future if people believe collaborating with us is a death sentence?" The young protégé ran a hand through his hair in exasperation.

"Let's take a deep breath and work the problem," Fahey said. "Remember your training. Remember when you landed your F-18 with two of its wheels shot off onto the USS Nimitz? Don't get emotional; stay focused," Fahey advised in a paternal tone as they arrived at FBI Headquarters.

★★★

CIA Director of Operations Tom Fahey never had any children of his own. His wife May Chiu suffered from a condition that made pregnancy impossible. Despite their happy marriage, a noticeable sadness hung over the couple that never seemed to go away except when Jim Keenan was around. The Faheys had been like second parents to the young man ever since he had been recruited to the CIA, and Keenan for his part was very much like the son they never had. He learned a great deal from his boss about the importance of communication, strategy, and organization, which enhanced his work at the Agency.

Keenan was a frequent guest at the Fahey home in Alexandria, Virginia. The two men thoroughly enjoyed each other's company, whether hunting, golfing, or having long conversations about world events over martinis. Fahey had shown his protégé how to be a successful spy. Keenan gave his mentor a sense of purpose beyond the Agency. The two had developed a friendship forged in trust, loyalty, and mutual respect, and in the precarious world of the clandestine service, that meant something.

★★★

The primary mission of the FBI's counterintelligence division is to identify and neutralize ongoing threats from foreign intelligence agencies, including the apprehension of spies inside the United States. After minimal chitchat, Keenan and Fahey entered the main conference room on the third floor that was already buzzing with activity.

Wentworth had arrived early and was having a sidebar conversation with FBI Head, Susan Kendall. She wore a gray Bloomingdale's pantsuit and listened patiently to Wentworth's pre-game version of events.

"Come in, gentlemen," FBI Deputy Director Richard Holmes bellowed from the far end of a long mahogany conference table. Holmes was a likable lawyer turned FBI agent from Los Angeles. He had a small build with short brown hair and a slightly tanned complexion resulting from his golf addiction. Sitting around him at the table were six counterintelligence team members who all stood from their chairs as the two men entered the room.

"Gents, I believe you know everyone here except for Special Agent Laura Bowman. Laura joined us a few months ago from the Criminal Investigative Division. She brings a wealth of knowledge and expertise to this situation."

As the teams made their rounds of shaking hands and saying hello, Keenan found himself transfixed on the keenly attractive Agent Bowman. She wore a perfectly fitted black skirt just above the knee with a white blouse, matching black blazer, and high heels, all of which accentuated her long brown hair, piercing green eyes, and toned legs. *Probably a runner*, Keenan surmised. He pulled back the empty chair next to Bowman and introduced himself, noticing an FDNY 9-11 memorial lapel pin on her jacket.

"Pardon my inquiry, Ms. Bowman; I was noticing your pin there. Did you lose someone on 9-11?" Keenan asked softly through the bustle of everyone taking their seats.

"My father," she replied. "He was the Battalion Chief at a firehouse in Midtown Manhattan that morning. They never found him. They never found any of them. Fifteen men, the entire shift, lost." Her tone, though flat, was polite. "I understand. My dad was on United 175 that morning," Keenan whispered back, just as the meeting began.

"Director Wentworth, Director Kendall, thank you both for joining us this morning," Holmes began. "Jim, do you want to kick us off with a PROJECT LUCY update?"

Jim Keenan stood and walked to the head of the conference room in front of a large television screen projecting his presentation. He picked up a small laser pointer off the table.

"Thanks for your time this morning," Keenan started without delay. "Our Chief of Station in Beijing has confirmed the execution of Pilgrim, another asset from our PROJECT LUCY operation in China. We're now certain that we have a mole in the Agency." He paused to let this sink in and then continued. "Pilgrim is the twelfth asset to be killed over the last six months. We still have eight assets working in China who we believe are alive but who are now completely exposed and in danger. These brave men and women are taking incredible risks because they believe in freedom. They believe in democracy. And they believe in our ability to protect them ," he said, pointing to eight nameless Chinese headshots on the TV screen behind him.

"I take it your team has found something of interest, Dick?" Fahey asked from across the table, looking in the direction of his FBI counterpart Richard Holmes.

"We think so, Tom. Ms. Bowman will take us through what we know so far."

Special Agent Bowman stood, buttoned her blazer, and walked to the front of the room where Keenan was still standing. He watched her approach before awkwardly realizing that he now needed to sit down.

"Good morning, everyone," she said in a calm and confident voice. "We want to bring you up to speed on an investigation we've been conducting over the last several months on one of your former analysts named Henry Kwok." Kwok's photo suddenly appeared on the video screen. "As you know, he was fired from the Agency last year."

Keenan's face lit up with surprise as Bowman aimed a laser pointer at Kwok's photo. He shook his head in disbelief as he fixed his stare on the man he had recruited, trained, and ultimately fired. *Could Henry Kwok really be a double agent?*

Bowman continued as she glanced around the table, "Agent Kwok was fired by the Agency due to drinking and gambling problems."

While Bowman continued to present her segment, thoughts raced through Keenan's head, recalling his years of working with Kwok and the friendship they had developed. In the spy business, drinking and gambling issues presented serious risks because those were the vices, along with sex addiction, that foreign intelligence services could best exploit when recruiting double agents.

Bowman continued, "Our team determined after reviewing Mr. Kwok's records at the time of his dismissal that he fit the high-risk profile that we look for, particularly his penchant for running up large gambling debts. Our suspicion was supported by a series of phone calls we traced between Mr. Kwok and persons in Hong Kong and Beijing together with his sudden preference for using prepaid phone cards. We began surveilling him closely to try and identify any attempts by foreign intelligence networks to flip him," Bowman said.

Keenan gave Tom Fahey a quick, concerned glance from across the table.

Fahey shot him a glance right back.

"We also discovered that Mr. Kwok's Bank of America account in Alexandria, Virginia, received two wire transfers from the HSBC Bank in Hong Kong in the amount of $9999.00 each. That dollar amount is, of course, suspect, because under the Bank Secrecy Act of 1970, banks are required to report deposits of $10,000 dollars or more to the IRS. These deposits to Kwok's account were meant to slide under the compliance radar."

Keenan gave another concerned glance at his boss.

"The two wire transfers," Bowman continued, "coincided with a $20,000 gambling debt that Kwok had run up playing blackjack at the Mohegan Sun Resort & Casino in Connecticut." A picture of the casino invoice appeared on the video screen.

"Could the bank deposits have come from any of Kwok's family members in Asia?" Fahey inquired. "If I recall correctly, he was born in Hong Kong and comes from a fairly wealthy family."

"If I may, Sir," Bowman interrupted, "there is a lot more material to get through that will paint a pretty clear picture of what we're looking at. Happy to answer questions after."

"My apologies, Ms. Bowman; please proceed."

"Thank you, Sir."

"Last month Kwok accepted a job as Chief Security Officer at Rothchild's Auction House in Hong Kong. As you know, the Agency will only verify employment dates of former agents to prospective employers. No information was given about his job performance while at the Agency, so he passed their background check. He relocated his wife and three children from their condominium in Alexandria, Virginia, to Hong Kong. On the way to Asia, Kwok took his family to Bali for a vacation. Our counterintelligence team entered the family's hotel room and searched his luggage while they were out to dinner. Since Kwok was permanently relocating to Hong Kong, we had a hunch that he would pack any sensitive documentation related to espionage activities and take it all with him."

Photos of Kwok's room at the Marriott Hotel in Bali appeared on the video screen, and Bowman drew everyone's attention to a particular item with a red laser pointer.

"Our agents found this notebook inside Kwok's leather carry-on bag. The first few pages of the notebook contained a list of names and phone numbers written in Chinese. Our agents took photos of the notebook pages and put it back into his carry-on bag. We didn't have a translator onsite, so we didn't know exactly what we were looking at. We contacted Deputy Director Holmes, and the decision was made to let Kwok and his family proceed to Hong Kong so that we could monitor his movements and see where he might lead us."

Holmes spoke up. "Seemed like the best decision, Tom. We couldn't hold him just for having a notebook of Chinese names, and we thought he would lead us to something bigger."

"It was the right call, Dick," Fahey replied.

Keenan's face had grown painfully anxious in anticipation. "And the notebook pages?" he inquired in a low voice.

Holmes produced a manila folder marked "TOP SECRET" and slid it across the conference room table to where Keenan was sitting.

He opened it slowly and began reading the names and phone numbers of every PROJECT LUCY asset he had in China, twelve of whom were already dead.

Everyone in the room respectfully waited for some type of reaction.

"Fuck," Keenan finally blurted out loud, confirming the names in disbelief.

"A great piece of detective work, Dick, and a clear summary of the situation, Ms. Bowman," Fahey said, trying to move the conversation to something less embarrassing and more forward looking. "So, is Kwok still in Hong Kong?"

"Yes," replied Holmes. "He is still there and working for Rothchild."

Wentworth finally spoke up. "Director Kendall, with your approval we'll need to have your team ready to join us in briefing the President sometime this afternoon."

"No problem, Charles; our team is ready whenever you are," the FBI Director replied quickly.

The meeting abruptly ended in an urgent but somber tone with the noise of participants standing and follow-up chatter around the room.

"PROJECT LUCY is blown," Keenan said to his mentor on the way out the door.

Fahey put a reassuring hand on his friend's shoulder and didn't say a word. He didn't have to.

POTUS

CHAPTER 6

The White House Situation Room: Washington D.C.

President Robert Blakely (POTUS) glanced impatiently at the door as he sat in the Situation Room wearing a white polo shirt emblazed with the presidential seal. The weather report was exceptional for July in Washington, and his motorcade waited outside to take him to The Congressional Country Club in Maryland for a round of golf. The Club was busy on weekends, but as the leader of the free world, no tee time was required.

First-time visitors to the Situation Room are amazed by how small it is, given the enormity of the decisions made there. The Sit Room, as it is known, was first established by President Kennedy after the Bay of Pigs disaster. White House staff members referred to it as the *Wizzar* from its initials, WHSR. Located downstairs from the West Wing basement entrance just across from the White House cafeteria, the Sit Room, with its five watch teams and thirty full-time National Security staff, provided the President and his National Security Adviser with intelligence and communications support around the clock.

The President sat at the head of the Sit Room's conference table, facing a quadrant of eight television screens. The oak table sat thirteen people somewhat uncomfortably. Additional chairs lined the walls on each side of the room for observers and support staff.

Blakely was seventy-one years old from Dothan Alabama. He was in the third year of his first term in office and was in surprisingly good health for a man who thrived on soft drinks, Doritos, and peanut butter cookies. He had never been to the White House gym and wasn't even sure where it was located.

A venture capitalist by profession, he had made billions investing in technology startup companies in Silicon Valley and later converted those billions into a real estate empire. In business, he witnessed first-hand China's disregard for intellectual property rights, human rights, the rule of law, and open markets. He had nothing against the Chinese people; his anger and contempt lay squarely with the corrupt one-party regime that ruled in Beijing. It was his personal quest to squash China and maintain America's global preeminence.

Blakely had campaigned on the promise of ending America's longstanding wars in the Middle East. He ordered the withdrawal of U.S. troops from Afghanistan, Syria, and Iraq in his first one hundred days in office—a catastrophic decision that created a power vacuum across the Middle East and spawned a violent resurgence of Al-Qaeda terrorist activity around the world.

Blakely's unorthodox methods in dealing with foreign leaders created friction and animosity between the U.S. and its longstanding allies. His unilateral approach to canceling treaties, starting trade wars, increasing sanctions, and supporting regime change in Iran and North Korea made the world a more volatile place in the eyes of western democracies. Blakely couldn't have cared less about what the rest of the world thought. He doubled down on economic sanctions against Iran, and he wasn't shy about launching Tomahawk missiles into the homes and automobiles of known Al-Qaeda leaders across the Middle East. On his desk inside the Oval Office was a simple wooden plaque that read "It's Us or Them."

FBI Director Susan Kendall and CIA Director Charles Wentworth took their seats on either side of the President at the Sit Room table, followed by Richard Holmes, Tom Fahey, Laura Bowman, and Jim Keenan. The NSA's Steven Berger and Secretary of Defense Lindsey Metcalf took their seats as well. A slew of support staff and note-takers sat along the Sit Room's perimeter. Those who couldn't find a seat, stood.

"What do we have this morning?" POTUS asked abruptly in kicking off the meeting.

Jim Keenan stood and walked with purpose to the front of the room, faced the President, and began the briefing. "Mr. President, the CIA has been implementing your

Executive Order 231, which calls for the technological containment of China, by running a top-secret operation called PROJECT LUCY. Our main objective, Sir, has been to gather actionable intelligence regarding Beijing's 'Made in China 2025' initiative." Keenan paused for a reaction from the President. There wasn't any. "Sir," Keenan continued, "we successfully recruited twenty Chinese Nationals working across various technology sectors inside Mainland China to provide us with information. We began collecting valuable intelligence almost immediately." Keenan paused again and deduced that the President's attention was divided between the meeting and his upcoming golf game. "As you know from your daily intelligence briefs, PROJECT LUCY assets began disappearing one by one about six months ago. They were later confirmed to have been executed."

Keenan suddenly had the President's attention as he perked up and began to focus.

"Sir, our Beijing Station Chief has confirmed that Pilgrim, our most valuable asset, has just been executed at Shanghai's Talinqiao Prison."

POTUS took a sip of coffee from the white mug next to him. "And what exactly do you think this means, Agent Keenan?"

"Sir, it means we have a mole inside the CIA, and thanks to the excellent work by the FBI's counterintelligence team," he said, looking over at Holmes and Bowman, "we believe the mole has been identified."

"And who is this shit bag?" POTUS asked in a calm but lethal tone.

"Sir, let me hand it over to Special Agent Bowman from the FBI to take you through what we know."

Keenan remembered to sit down this time as Laura Bowman took center stage. Admiring her calm demeanor and physical presence, Keenan again felt he had been caught staring at her just a little too long.

"Good morning, Mr. President," she began. "Henry Kwok was a CIA analyst working inside PROJECT LUCY." A picture of Kwok appeared on the large TV screen in the center of the wall behind her. "Mr. Kwok was a heavy drinker with a gambling addiction."

"Nice combination," POTUS chimed in.

"Yes, Sir," she continued. "Kwok began going on long drinking binges while racking up large gambling debts at various East Coast casinos. When the Agency learned of his behavior, he was placed on probation, and after numerous second chances, he was finally let go."

"And what happens to a CIA agent that gets fired?" POTUS asked.

"Sir, whenever an agent is let go under these circumstances, the FBI's counterintelligence unit conducts careful surveillance for an unspecified amount of time to ensure foreign intelligence agencies don't try to recruit them."

Everyone listened attentively, and Tom Fahey nodded in agreement.

"Go on."

Bowman went on to explain the wire transfers Kwok received from Hong Kong, and his sudden relocation to Asia.

"That only means he's a drunk gambler with a rich connection in Hong Kong, Ms. Bowman. It doesn't prove he's a rat or a mole or whatever you call them, does it?" POTUS leaned forward, his arms crossed on the table.

Bowman then focused on Kwok's trip to Bali and the notebook that was found in his hotel room containing the names of assets in China.

"Mr. President, Henry Kwok is the mole," she concluded.

"Son of a bitch," POTUS blurted, his face contorted in agitation.

As Bowman returned to her seat, it was FBI Deputy Director Richard Holmes's turn to lead the discussion. He did so from his chair. "Mr. President, Kwok is now working legitimately for Rothchild's Auction House in Hong Kong as their new head of cybersecurity. We believe he gets a substantial payout from Beijing for each CIA asset he delivers to the Chinese, and given the spacing of the executions in China, it appears he delivers two names per month. We need to stop him as quickly as possible to save the Agency's eight remaining assets."

"What do you propose we do, Dick?" POTUS asked intently.

The discussion switched to FBI Director Susan Kendall, a distinguished woman of sixty-three with a small face and brown tortoiseshell glasses, the first female director of the Bureau. She possessed a Rain Man-like ability to analyze and process complicated data. When she spoke, everyone paid attention.

"Mr. President, we need to bring Henry Kwok back to the United States as quickly as possible," Kendall said. "The problem, Sir, is that we no longer have an extradition treaty with Hong Kong. The streets are still on fire over there, and young protestors are being rounded up by the PLA. China has also implemented a new national security law in Hong Kong. They have essentially reneged on the Sino-British Joint Declaration of 1984," Kendall concluded.

"It's another damn Cold War with these Chinese," the President said.

"And Hong Kong is the new Berlin. Caught right smack in the middle of East and West," said Tom Fahey.

"You know we're revoking Hong Kong's special trading status with the Unites States next week, and we're sanctioning Hong Kong's government leaders personally in response to all their human rights bullshit, so whatever we're going to do over there, we'd better do it fast," POTUS demanded. "What's the recommendation?"

Fahey spoke up. "Mr. President, our plan is to send Agents Keenan and Bowman over to Hong Kong tonight as a first step. They will follow Kwok for a few days and see if he leads us to his Beijing handler. We believe he meets with this handler regularly."

Director Kendall added, "In parallel, we will meet with Rothchild executives and get them to initiate a business trip for Mr. Kwok under the guise of his giving a security presentation to their office in New York. When Kwok lands in New York and clears immigration, we can arrest him on the spot."

"Chuck, are you good with this?" the President asked his CIA Director.

"We believe it's the cleanest option. Rothchild doesn't want anything to impact their valuable reputation, so they will cooperate."

"And you, Dick?"

"Yes, Sir, good here."

"Susan?"

"It's our best option, Sir."

POTUS stood from his seat, and everyone in the room reflexively stood with him. "Okay, let's do this," he said, turning toward the door. "Nail the son of a bitch." When Blakely got to the door to leave, he stopped and turned back to address the group. "You've probably heard, I'm in the middle of a political shit storm with my re-election campaign at the moment. And since all your jobs depend on me keeping mine, don't fuck this up."

As the President exited, Laura Bowman leaned in toward Keenan. "Is he always this eloquent?" she whispered with a grin.

On the main television screen at the front of the Situation Room, a staff member turned the volume up on a breaking CNN news report from the White House lawn.

> "Leaders across the international community openly voiced their concerns with the Blakely Administration today during

a special meeting of the U.N. Security Council in New York. 'Treaties have been cancelled, trade wars have been implemented, and protectionist policies are now running rampant,' said one high-level official who asked not to be identified. The Blakely Administration's unilateral withdrawal from the Iranian nuclear deal and the imposition of even tougher sanctions against Tehran are counter-productive, say many world leaders. 'He is antagonizing dangerous enemies, and we can expect terrorist activities will increase as a result,' said British Prime Minister Stanley Hanover. *This is Josh Rosiner reporting live from the White House.*"

NOTHING TO LOSE

CHAPTER 7

Port of Gwadar, Balochistan Province, Pakistan

On a late afternoon outside an abandoned warehouse in Pakistan's Port of Gwadar, Al-Qaeda 's top military strategist arrived in a dusty gray SUV. Abdul Saleem got out of his car timidly, surrounded by his security team. He looked to the left and right through his green-tinted Ray-Ban sunglasses to survey any potential threats. It was a habit he'd developed from years of nefarious field work.

Saleem was tall and lanky with a long, thin face, graying beard, and bushy black eyebrows. Crow's feet framed his dark and serious eyes. A deep worry line ran across the forehead. The experienced soldier wore a traditional white thobe and sandals with a matching keffiyeh headdress. He had come to Gwadar to meet with his Iranian Revolutionary Guard contact he called Darzi. They had met twice before on other matters—in Damascus and

Tehran. He admired Darzi's direct and purposeful manner. On this hot afternoon, the sun beat down from a clear blue sky and Saleem felt anxious.

The uneasy relationship between Al-Qaeda and Iran was one of strategic convenience based on the proverb, *the enemy of my enemy is my friend.* They shared a common hatred for the United States and Israel, wanting to see both destroyed. Iran provided safe haven for Al-Qaeda operatives after the attacks on 9-11, and over the years allowed Al-Qaeda to establish its operational headquarters in the country.

Saleem knew the economic situation in Iran had become untenable. U.S. sanctions were crushing the Iranian economy, and something had to be done. Iran viewed Al-Qaeda as a valuable proxy for waging war against its oppressors in Washington. Recent discussions between Iran and Al-Qaeda focused on expanding the relationship—allowing the terrorist group access to Iran's satellite networks, intelligence data, military training, and weapons to bolster their effort against America. Saleem hoped that today Iran would agree to take a heroic next step.

He was led into the abandoned warehouse by one of Darzi's personal bodyguards through a large, gray sliding door that looked like it hadn't been opened for decades. The location wasn't unusual. Meetings like this rarely took place at a Four Seasons Hotel.

"As-Salaam Alaikum," the tall man greeted Darzi warmly.

"Wa Alaikum as-Salaam," came an equally warm reply.

Darzi was of average height but heavy for his frame. Just fifty-nine, his yellowish complexion, unshaven face, and tired, bloodshot eyes made him look much older. He was dressed like most Iranian government officials, wearing a white band collared shirt and a simple blue blazer which he wore despite the oppressive heat.

The warehouse reeked of oil and gasoline from long-abandoned machinery. The heavy odor was magnified by the late afternoon temperature. The office area was dimly lit by a single lightbulb dangling from the ceiling by an exposed electrical wire. An aging air conditioner groaned laboriously from an office window, blowing a warm breeze across the stuffy room. Saleem took a seat across from Darzi in an old wooden chair that had been hastily wiped cleaned for the meeting.

Given the uncomfortable conditions, Saleem thought it best to skip the pleasantries and get right to the point. "Brother Darzi, I thank you for coming to Pakistan and seeing me on such short notice. I've come to tell you that we are prepared to launch a new attack on the United States," he began, "an attack that will dwarf September 11th."

Darzi listened impassively, legs crossed. "That's a bold statement, my good friend. The 9-11 attack was an historic success." He paused to take a puff of his cigarette. "But you have my attention, brother, so please continue."

"We understand that you have been able to secretly develop a number of tactical nuclear weapons as part of your AMAD research initiative, and you have somehow kept these weapons hidden from the U.N. inspection teams," Saleem said with confidence.

An uncomfortable pause lingered as the two men studied each other in silence. Darzi gave nothing away. His mind flashed back to AQ Khan, the father of Pakistan's nuclear program, who sold his nuclear blueprints to Tehran many years before famously delivering the plans in a plastic bag he got from his tailor in Islamabad.

Saleem continued, "We also know that Israeli commandos broke into your Parchin military base two weeks ago and confiscated documents that confirm the existence of your nuclear weapons."

Another blank stare from Darzi.

"And we hear through our sources that the Israelis are actively looking for these weapons using Mossad commando teams inside Iran."

"My friend, you seem to have a lot of information," Darzi finally responded in frustration over the leaks coming from his own intelligence team.

"We would like to help you, brother," Saleem interjected before Darzi had the chance to become angry.

With a slight air of superiority, Darzi asked, "And how would *you* propose to help me, brother?"

"We would like to purchase your nuclear devices and use them to attack the United States," Saleem said with a defusing grin.

Darzi stubbed out his cigarette on the decrepit table. He stroked his unshaven face and contemplated what he had just heard. Life had not been easy for Darzi. He was tired of the inept Iranian government. Tired of U.S. sanctions that made his family's life miserable. He was tired of being tired. He knew Saleem's intelligence was entirely correct and that it was only a matter of time before the Israelis found the weapons they were looking for. When that day came, he knew life in Iran would become exponentially worse with further retaliation by the West.

Lighting another cigarette, Darzi said, "Tell me what you have in mind brother," taking a long drag and blowing smoke toward the ceiling.

Saleem relaxed, sensing a positive reaction. "We will cripple their economy with two blows," he began. "America's supply chain is its Achilles heel. It's as porous as that screen door," he said, pointing to the office entry. "Our plan is to transport two nuclear weapons to America using two separate container ships. One vessel will go to the Port of Los Angeles, and the other will sail through the Panama Canal on its way to New York. We will detonate the first bomb inside the Panama Canal, followed by a second detonation in downtown Los Angeles. Then we will take responsibility for the attacks through global news agencies."

Darzi considered the enormity of the plan as he finished his cigarette, squishing the butt beneath his shoe. *The Panama Canal would be out of commission for years, forcing cargo ships to transit all the way around Cape Horn on the southern tip of South America. International trade would come to a halt. Global financial markets would crash. The United States economy would shut down with fear, panic, and rioting. It would create total anarchy, and it would be beautiful to watch*, Darzi thought. Then he contemplated the consequences of what the U.S. would do to Iran if Saleem's attack were ever linked back to Tehran.

Iran would need an iron-clad alibi to ensure there could be no connection to such an attack. Darzi carefully worked out various scenarios in his head. The solution came to him quickly, and his dark eyes widened, indicating he had an idea.

Noticing a change in the other man's expression, Saleem spoke up. "So, you will sell us the weapons? We are prepared to pay whatever price you ask."

After a thoughtful moment Darzi sat upright in his chair and leaned across the table. "No, my friend. That would be impossible. Selling you these weapons would be far too risky."

Saleem's tall body slumped. He sat quietly, looking down at the floor.

"However, brother," Darzi continued, "I will make it possible for you to steal the weapons."

Saleem grinned, immediately recognizing the genius of Darzi's solution.

"We will get details to you on where the weapons are being stored, and we will make sure the path is clear for your operation," Darzi said.

Saleem stood and reached across the table. "Allahu Akbar," he said, grasping and shaking the hand of Darzi, who likewise stood.

God is great.

BURIED TREASURE

CHAPTER 8

Persepolis, Zagros Mountains, Iran

The Zagros Mountains of Iran stretch for over 1,000 miles, creating a barricade between antiquity and the modern world. In these mountains stands the ancient city of Persepolis. Built by Darius the Great in 515 BC, the former capital of Persia was eventually sacked by Alexander in a dramatic clash between East and West. The ancient city was declared an UNESCO World Heritage Site, its treasures carefully unearthed by the country's National History Museum.

For Iran's Revolutionary Guard the excavation site at Persepolis offered more than historical treasure. The site provided credible cover, beyond the suspicion of western intelligence agencies. Persepolis was the perfect place to hide the country's secret nuclear weapons.

★★★

The nighttime sky above Persepolis beamed brightly under a white crescent moon as the Al-Qaeda commandos, led by Abdul Saleem's brother Rajiv, arrived in two cargo trucks and a black Range Rover. Under normal circumstances the moonlit conditions would be too risky for such a clandestine operation. But on this night, the moon provided welcomed visibility and would speed up operations considerably.

Iran's Islamic Revolutionary Guard normally patrolled the site, but Darzi made sure all his patrols had taken the night off. The Al-Qaeda caravan drove through the site's entry gate, which had been intentionally left open, and entered Persepolis without notice or interference at 2300 hours, exactly as planned.

The vehicles came to a stop in front of a storage facility just inside the gate. Rajiv got out of his Range Rover and began scanning the grounds. He was shorter than his brother Saleem but just as thin, with an olive complexion and a jet-black beard. He wore dark, military-style clothing, including a black knit hat, climbing boots, a communications headset, and a backpack. The rest of the six-man team dressed in similar fashion and carried AK-47's.

The gray cinderblock storage facility had been constructed to house excavation equipment. Electrical generators noisily churned inside, providing electricity. From ground level the facility appeared to be just one story high, but deep beneath the building's floor lay a large vault where the nuclear weapons were being stored. It had been secretly constructed under the noses of western spy satellites. Even the Israelis had missed it.

With the Al-Qaeda commando team in place, the staged robbery began with the aggressive application of bolt cutters on the facility's padlocked doors. Inside, Rajiv turned on his headlamp, and the rest of his team did the same.

"Test—test," Rajiv said into his headset microphone.

His men all gave a thumb's up.

Rajiv looked at the warehouse blueprints, courtesy of Darzi, and pointed in the direction of the freight elevator on the northern side of the building that would take them to the storage room beneath. They located it in the corner, a large hydraulic lift with a manual pull-down door.

"Ahmed, come with me," Rajiv said to his second in command. "The rest of you stay here. We're going down to have a look." The two men entered the elevator, their headlamp beams crisscrossing each other in the dark. Ahmed pulled the door down to close it.

Rajiv deduced that the lower knob was the down button and pushed it. The elevator's hydraulic system sprang to life with a low groan of machinery in motion. An odor of hydraulic fluid wafted through the dank air as they slowly descended, like coal miners from a bygone era.

The elevator stopped at the bottom with a small thump, and Rajiv opened the door. Down a wide, dimly lit hallway they could see green and red electronic lights flickering on the storage vault's security access mechanism. As they approached the vault door, Rajiv took off his backpack and placed it on the floor. Reaching inside, he took out a zip-lock bag containing a man's amputated right hand, his headlamp illuminating the appendage's badly serrated wrist and a montage of dried blood, white bone, and shards of dangling skin.

"What the fuck is that?" Ahmed exclaimed, staring at the bag's gruesome contents.

"According to my brother Saleem, there are only three nuclear engineers in Iran who have the fingerprints needed to access this room," Rajiv replied. "Brother Darzi decided that one of those engineers needed to sacrifice a hand to help sell this operation as a robbery."

"They made that poor bastard suffer," Ahmed replied. "That's a real hack job." Ahmed had seen many body parts chopped off in his difficult life and considered himself somewhat of an expert.

"It's supposed to look violent for effect," Rajiv replied.

Wearing rubber gloves, Rajiv took the severed hand out of the plastic bag and placed its five fingers on the glass touch pad as best he could. A red scanner beam automatically moved slowly up and down the glass pad, reading the macabre fingerprints. It was a gamble, Rajiv knew. Sometimes these scanners needed to sense the heat of the human fingers in order to properly read the fingerprints. Rajiv thought the owner of the hand had probably made the same argument before it was brutally hacked off. The vault's door mechanism noisily engaged, the internal bolts sliding to the unlocked position. A wisp of escaping air could be heard as the hermetically sealed door opened, and pressure from the two sides of the door equalized.

"Okay, we're in," Rajiv said into his headset mic.

The storage room's sensor lights turned on automatically as the two men entered. The area was temperature controlled with cool air blowing through the ceiling vents thanks to the running generators. In the middle of the room sat two large, identical wooden crates. Each crate was labeled "Magnetic Resonance Imaging Equipment" in large black lettering and "HANDLE WITH CARE - THIS SIDE UP" stenciled in bold red lettering. It was the perfect disguise for the nuclear weapons which were similar in size, weight, and radioactive signature to an MRI machine. Attached to each crate was a pouch containing authorized sets of shipping documents and commercial invoices which would be needed to ship the crates internationally. Brother Darzi had thought of everything.

"Okay, we've located *Romeo* and *Juliet*," Rajiv advised the team. "We'll need to get a couple of those forklifts started up there."

The entire process took less than forty-five minutes. Each crate was taken up in the freight elevator and loaded onto a truck. They were covered with black and green waterproof tarps and tied down with heavy rope.

"Let's make sure this looks like a robbery," Rajiv reminded everyone over the radio.

Bolt cutters and other tools were left scattered about. The severed hand was well positioned on the floor just beneath the security access pad so it would be easily found by investigators.

Rajiv again stooped down and reached into his backpack as Ahmed looked on, afraid of what his friend would pull out of his bag this time. It was an Israeli IDF commando helmet.

"What's that for?" Ahmed inquired.

"It's a request from Darzi. We need to leave this helmet behind."

"Why?"

"So when Iranian government officials bring in the western media they can point to the Israeli helmet as proof the Jews stole their nukes."

"Well, isn't that just brilliant?" Ahmed replied with a smile.

As the operation came to an end, Rajiv assigned two drivers per truck for the six-hundred-kilometer trek from Persepolis to the Iranian seaport of Bandar Abbas. The trip would take eight hours, with each driver doing a four-hour shift. Rajiv would follow in the Range Rover in case there was a problem. He gathered his men in a circle before departure, their headlamp beams crisscrossing like light sabers in the night.

"Tonight, we go with God," Rajiv said to them. "This Jihad against our visible enemies will change the world forever. Praise Allah."

As the caravan set out for Bandar Abbas, clouds began to cover the crescent moon, and the darkness provided exceptional cover for the moving convoy.

"It is a good omen," Rajiv whispered to himself. "Praise Allah."

BON VOYAGE

CHAPTER 9

Bandar Abbas, Iran

In the early morning hours following a long night's drive, Rajiv's secret caravan arrived at the Iranian seaport of Bandar Abbas. Strategically located on the Straits of Hormuz, the Iranian port sits at the epicenter of Middle Eastern oil exports and is home to the Islamic Revolutionary Guard's naval forces.

The two cargo trucks were guided into a large government-owned distribution center located just inside the port's heavily patrolled perimeter. They drove directly into the building through a large metal garage door that immediately closed behind them. The two shipping crates were carefully offloaded by a forklift and gently placed on the polished floor. The facility was empty except for the Pakistani nuclear technicians who were awaiting the caravan's arrival. Darzi had been meticulous in his arrangements.

The technicians carefully opened the packing crates and began the work of arming each weapon with cell-phone-activated triggering devices. "Hard to believe you can kill a million people with just a phone call," Rajiv said to Ahmed as the two watched the delicate arming procedure.

"You know, Rajiv, the Americans kill people remotely, too," Ahmed said, sensing Rajiv's conscience was kicking in. "They murder using drone strikes and economic sanctions. They feel better about themselves by not getting their hands dirty. But it's still murder."

Rajiv nodded quietly.

It took less than an hour for the nuclear technicians to complete the triggering process and to reassemble the shipping crates. Each box was placed inside its own steel cargo container. The identification number of each container was well documented by Ahmed before the boxes were trucked out to the shipping dock. Twelve red and white cargo cranes, each over three hundred feet tall dominated the Bandar Abbas skyline. The bomb containers were hoisted high into the air and over the ship's railing before being placed gently onboard the IRISIL *Pasha*, a small Iranian flag cargo ship operated by the Iranian government.

The voyage from Bandar Abbas to China would be the riskiest part of the plan and where Darzi knew he would be most exposed. Using a foreign flag shipping line would have been the best solution for such a secret operation, but under U.S. sanctions, foreign shipping companies were forbidden to do business in Iran. China was one of the few places where Iranian ships were still allowed to enter.

'So, what happens from here?" Ahmed asked Rajiv as the two men stood looking up at the cargo ship.

"The *Pasha* will sail to the Port of Shanghai. Once there, the crates will be trans-loaded onto two separate container ships bound for the United States. The crews of those ships will have no knowledge of our plan or what they are carrying. Brother Darzi has provided forged customs and shipping documentation to make it look like these are medical devices being shipped to hospitals in the United States."

"And when the bombs are in position, we set them off with a phone call?" Ahmed asked.

"Yes, praise Allah."

As the sun set over Bandar Abbas, the IRISIL *Pasha* slipped its moorings and quietly steamed out of the harbor. It headed east for the six-thousand-five-hundred nautical mile journey to Shanghai. At an average speed of twenty knots, and weather permitting, the *Pasha* would arrive in China in fourteen days, in plenty of time to connect with the intended ships heading to the United States.

Rajiv left the port in his Range Rover with his friend Ahmed behind the wheel. He was pleased the operation had been so successful. It had been more than twenty hours since he had last slept and the mission's adrenaline had long since worn off. He texted his brother Saleem with a pre-set code to advise that the two bombs were on their way to Shanghai. "*Romeo and Juliet are on the balcony.*"

The only thing left to do was to text the triggering device phone numbers to their Al-Qaeda contacts in Panama and Los Angeles. He carefully typed each phone number on WhatsApp while Ahmed tried to keep the ride smooth. He double checked that each phone number matched the assigned triggers for both *Romeo* and *Juliet* and then hit 'Send.' "Well, that's that," he mumbled to himself.

The attack on America was officially underway, and his team had performed flawlessly. Rajiv leaned back in his seat, rested his head, and closed his eyes. He whispered, "Praise Allah" and fell into a deep and peaceful slumber.

HIDE AND SEEK

CHAPTER 10

Mossad Headquarters – Tel Aviv, Israel

Israel's Mossad is the fiercest intelligence agency in the world. It has to be. In a country surrounded by enemies, Israel's survival depends on having the best intelligence by whatever means necessary. Spycraft, data gathering, innovative technologies, and a brazen history of liquidating enemies of the Israeli State—nobody did it better.

On the fifth floor of Mossad headquarters in Tel Aviv, Director Shai Cohen called a meeting of his top lieutenants together with General Benjamin Green, who headed Sayeret Matkal, the commando unit of the Israel Defense Forces (IDF). Cohen, who had been an IDF commando in his younger years, was now in his late fifties, still with the physique of a marathon runner. He stood at medium height with a balding head, a friendly face, and light blue eyes. Cohen hated wearing neck ties and did so poorly—his Windsor knots always askew to one side or the other.

Over his many years inside the global intelligence community, Cohen had become close friends with Tom Fahey at the CIA. Their careers were mirror images, following the same rapid upward trajectory. They spoke often by phone and occasionally vacationed together with their wives. Fahey served as sponsor to Cohen's son Robert at his Bar Mitzvah. And when Cohen's father passed away suddenly in New York, it was Tom Fahey who personally escorted the body back to Israel. The relationship between the two men personally and professionally helped to ensure that the two most powerful spy agencies in the world worked well together.

General Benjamin Green boisterously entered the meeting room. At six foot five, dressed in military khakis, he was a commanding physical presence in any setting. He went straight over to Cohen. The two shook hands and exchanged pleasantries as everyone took their seats.

"Gentlemen," Cohen began, "the raid that was conducted by our commando unit in Tehran last month left no doubt that the Iranians have developed at least two nuclear weapons." He looked around and continued, "As you know, Colonel David Glickman led the raid into Iran's Parchin Military compound and confiscated a safe that contained secret documents detailing every aspect of Iran's nuclear development program.

"Iran's code name for their nuke program is *Amad*," the General interjected for clarity.

"While the documents confirm the nuclear weapons exist, there was nothing to indicate where they were being hidden," Cohen continued. "We've spent the last several weeks combing satellite imagery and reading transcripts of bugged conversations inside Tehran's leadership, looking for clues."

"Anything so far?" General Green inquired.

"Yes," Cohen answered quickly. "There's an archeological excavation going on at the ancient city of Persepolis, located here," Cohen said, pointing to a spot on a map of southwestern Iran. "We knew about the site, but nothing on satellite imagery showed anything unusual for an archaeological dig."

"And a dig site like that would be a great location to hide things like nuclear weapons," the General again interjected.

"Exactly," Cohen replied.

Cohen continued, "Over the past week our listening posts started picking up the name 'Persepolis' being used repeatedly in Revolutionary Guard conversations and in Al-Qaeda chatter. We also began hearing *Romeo* and *Juliet* in government and Al-Qaeda conversations across multiple communication networks. Our artificial intelligence team ran the conversational data through an algorithm to identify patterns. Turns out the words 'weapon,' 'nuclear,' 'Amad,' along with 'Romeo and Juliet' are showing up in the same chatter sequences as the name Persepolis."

"Bingo," the General chimed in.

"Yes, and shame on us for not finding it sooner," Cohen said in chagrin.

"General, we need one of your commando units to go into Persepolis as soon as possible so we can find out what the fuck is going on in there," Cohen said sternly . "Ben, I know it's a rush ed job," Cohen said, "but can we get your team in there by tomorrow? If there are nukes being hidden there, we need them documented and destroyed on the spot."

"Can do. I'll use Colonel Glickman's tactical team again. I can have them here for a briefing in two hours."

"Thanks, Ben."

"That area is about 2100 kilometers from Tel Aviv," the General continued. "We can drop Glickman's team into Persepolis tonight with a low-level jump by plane and get them out using the helicopter evacuation team we keep in Kuwait," said the General.

The meeting quickly ended. Cohen called his friend Tom Fahey to fill him in on the day's developments and the upcoming operation. *If the shit hits the fan on this operation, the Americans will come in handy*, he thought.

★★★

At 0100 hours, Colonel Glickman and his team of six IDF commandos parachuted into the moonless night sky over Iran. By design they landed approximately two miles from the target site of Persepolis and began briskly hiking toward it. The team wore black uniforms, bulletproof vests, gloves, and armored helmets equipped with night vision goggles.

Their faces were covered by black paint and ski masks. Each carried an Israeli IMI UZI submachine gun.

Steven Bell served as the team's *wick*—the endearing term given to the soldier who carries the explosives. Glickman's helmet had a Go-Pro streaming camera attached, providing live coverage of the operation to the command center back in Tel Aviv.

Expecting a swath of Revolutionary Guard forces around the compound, they were surprised to find Persepolis unprotected. In fact, the site was completely abandoned.

Glickman checked his GPS to make sure they had the right coordinates. There were fresh tire tracks around the storage building, and the perimeter fence was open. Two industrial-size generators could be heard noisily providing electricity to the facility. This gave Glickman a ray of hope that they might find something here. *Why would a maintenance storage facility in the middle of nowhere need so much electricity?*

The commandos slowly approached the facility. Taking out their bolt cutters, they were surprised to find the facility's locks had already been cut.

"Something's not right," Glickman said into his microphone. "Are you seeing this, Center?"

"We see it, Colonel," came the reply from General Green back at headquarters. "Please proceed."

Inside the facility, the team gathered much the same way Rajiv's team had the night before. They did a radio check.

"We have sixty minutes to find and disable the nukes before our rendezvous with the chopper," the Colonel informed his team as they synchronized their watches. "If something goes wrong, and we're forced to scramble, we meet at rendezvous point Alpha at 0230 hours for chopper extraction. Understood?"

"Yes, Colonel," came the reply in unison.

The team donned their night vision goggles that made them look like aliens. "See if you can find some kind of elevator," Glickman ordered. "If they're hiding anything, it will be below us."

They began searching the facility.

"There," he said pointing to the elevator. "Lieutenant Abrams, on me. We're going down to have a look. Wick, you hold here with the rest of the team. I'll call you down when we're ready."

It was a repeat performance of the steps Rajiv and his team had taken the night before. Glickman closed the gate, and they slowly descended. "Are you seeing us, Control?"

"Roger, Colonel," came the reply from Center. "Looking good."

At the bottom of the elevator shaft, Lieutenant Abrams opened the cage door. They noticed a wave of cool air flowing out of a large, vault-like door directly in front of them. Heading down the wide hallway, they paused in front of the vault's security access pad. A severed hand lay on the ground just beneath it.

"Are you getting this, Control?"

"We copy."

"The vault door is wide open—looks like they used the handprint to gain access," Glickman said.

The commando team above gave one another inquisitive looks, listening on their radios to the play-by-play going on beneath them.

"Something's really fucked up here, General," came the warning from Glickman to his boss in Tel Aviv. The two men entered the storage room, and the lights came on automatically, temporarily blinding them in their night vision goggles.

"The fucking thing is empty," Glickman radioed. "It looks like the place has been robbed."

"Copy that, Colonel," said the General. "Get your team the hell out of there and proceed to the rendezvous point."

"Copy that."

"Oh, and Colonel."

"Sir?"

"Take the hand with you."

Glickman motioned to his young Lieutenant to collect the appendage.

"Prepare to exit," Glickman radioed his commandos. "We're coming up."

Back at Control in Tel Aviv, the leadership team sat stunned. Director Cohen and General Green looked at each other in silence. "If our assumptions are correct, gentlemen, the Iranians were able to develop at least two tactical nuclear weapons. They successfully hid them in Persepolis, and either the weapons have been moved because they knew we were coming—or they have been stolen."

"The Revolutionary Guard wouldn't have needed bolt cutters and an amputated hand if they just wanted to relocate their own weapons," Cohen remarked.

"So that leaves us with a very frightening scenario," the General said in a low and serious tone. "Someone has stolen Iran's nukes."

The conference room door opened suddenly, and Mossad's Assistant Director for Communications, Kenneth Kaplan, entered with a noticeable look of concern. He was followed by several members of his team.

"What is it, Ken?" Cohen asked.

"Sir, we've been monitoring Iranian military and government conversations very closely leading up to Colonel Glickman's operation."

"Yes, I know."

"Well, Sir, the intel we're getting from all the background chatter collected yesterday and today indicates that the nuclear devices Colonel Glickman is trying to find have been stolen. We can confirm from radio intercepts that there is a massive search going on right now by the Revolutionary Guard to try and find the weapons."

"Fuck," the General let slip.

"We'll need to notify the Prime Minister immediately. And our friends in Washington. We also need to initiate our highest-level security alert in case those nukes are heading our way," Cohen said.

"Rogue nukes. My god," Kaplan whispered to himself as he looked up at the wall-mounted television in the front of the conference room. "Hey, turn this up," he said, pointing to the screen as CNN was broadcasting *Breaking News.* Everyone in the room stared at the main television screen as Cohen's assistant turned up the volume.

> "CNN has learned from senior officials inside the State Department that an undetermined number of nuclear weapons illegally developed by Iran and secretly hidden in the country's Zagros Mountains have reportedly been stolen from an underground bunker beneath the ancient city of Persepolis. Iranian officials contacted CNN a short time ago to publicly blame Israel for the theft. They are demanding that the United Nations condemn this action as a violation of Iran's national sovereignty."

The conference room went silent until Ken Kaplan asked the question everyone had been thinking. "Why would Tehran finally admit to having developed nuclear weapons after denying it for so many years? And why would they be so eager to announce to the media that the weapons had been stolen?"

Director Cohen's face grew long as the scheme became clear. "Because Ken, Iran has figured out a way to move their weapons to a new hiding place while at the same time screwing Israel."

The room again went silent.

"The Iranians deliberately increased the chatter on Persepolis all across their networks, knowing that we were listening," Cohen continued. "We should have known it was a setup. They practically drove us to Persepolis in a fucking Uber. Get me the Prime Minister on the line," Cohen said to his assistant. "And then get me Tom Fahey at CIA."

Mossad was not accustomed to explaining mistakes or looking foolish. These were going to be difficult conversations.

SURVEILLANCE

CHAPTER 11

Special Administrative Region of Hong Kong China

Everyone thinks they have a cure for jet lag, Keenan thought as he gazed out the window of Cathay Pacific flight 881 and admired the early morning sunrise over the South China Sea. He'd heard all the remedies—when to stay awake, when to fall asleep, drink plenty of water, avoid alcohol on the flight, and set watches to the destination's time zone. It was all bullshit.

The human body is not designed to stay aloft at 40,000 feet for fifteen hours across twelve time zones, he mused. His jet lag formula for Asia flights was simple: a couple of Bloody Mary's after takeoff, a couple of glasses of red wine with dinner, a five-milligram dose of Ambien when the flight reached the halfway point across the Pacific. His routine ensured at least eight hours of sleep before the in-flight breakfast service began prior to arrival into Hong Kong .

Laura had chosen a more natural approach to jet lag prevention. She shunned the airplane cocktails and avoided sleeping pills. Instead, she drank copious amounts of water and rubbed jasmine oil on her wrists as a holistic sedative. That program was a complete failure. Over-hydration together with the cabin pressure on her bladder at forty thousand feet meant a trip to the restroom every hour. The jasmine oil didn't make her sleepy, but it did make her smell like an expensive spa, enhancing her effortless allure.

As the Cathay flight approached the coast of Macau it banked to the right, beginning its final approach into Hong Kong's Chek Lap Kok Airport. Flight attendants hastily cleared the business class breakfast service and prepared the plane for landing. An irritating cacophony of announcements and instructions from the chief purser wailed over the plane's intercom, first in English, then in Cantonese, and again in Mandarin, allowing passengers to completely ignore the instructions in three different languages.

The Boeing 777 gently touched down at 0602 hours and began the short taxi to the Cathay Pacific terminal. Keenan felt remarkably refreshed and was anxious to deplane. Putting his paperwork and computer back in his carry-on bag, he gazed out the window in anticipation of the day's events.

Laura's condition was not as promising. She'd managed only two hours of sleep and felt like she had been hit by a bus. Her muscles ached, and she experienced brain fog from sleep deprivation. She quickly ran a comb through her hair and tied it up in a bun as the plane arrived at the gate. The seatbelt sign bell rang loudly, giving the 'All clear' for the 388 passengers to open their overhead bins and begin moving toward the exits.

Keenan was off the plane first and waited for Laura at the end of the jetway bridge. He could see her walking toward him behind a slow-moving group of weary passengers, rolling her carry-on suitcase behind her. He was pleased there would be no baggage claim to deal with.

"Good flight?" Keenan asked as she approached.

"Well, Jim, let's just say I'm now caught up on all my movies," she answered in a tired but humorous tone.

"Look at the bright side, Laura. You can binge-watch *Game of Thrones* and the *Harry Potter* series on the way home," Keenan said with a sympathetic smile. As they walked toward the immigration hall, he caught the lingering scent of Jasmine, which he found quite appealing; it reminded him of a great spa he had once frequented in Thailand.

"I need to stop at the ladies' room before we get to immigration," she said, her hydration program continuing to flow through her system. The restroom was just around the corner.

As they proceeded through Immigration and into the airport's cavernous arrival hall, they spotted their driver, who had been sent by the U.S. Consulate, holding up a sign with their names printed on it.

"Welcome to Hong Kong, Mr. Keenan, Ms. Bowman. I'm Gary Lau," the driver said in perfect English as he reached over to help Laura with her bag.

"Jo San," Keenan replied, proud to have remembered the Cantonese phrase for "Good morning."

Gary gave a quick smile of acknowledgement to Keenan's language skills. "I'll be driving you both to your hotel to freshen up and then over to the Consulate later this morning," the short, dark-haired Chinese man said in an upbeat tone.

"Great, thank you," Laura replied.

With bags in tow, Gary took them down an escalator and outside to the short-term parking lot. There were only two types of weather temperature in Hong Kong—hot in the winter and unbearably hot in the summer. As the automatic doors opened to the parking lot, the ninety-degree July heat together with the oppressive humidity hit the new arrivals like a ton of bricks.

"My kingdom for a shower," Laura joked, getting into the Consulate van. The vehicle's air conditioner finally kicked on to provide relief. As the van cooled, she fell asleep and would miss the forty-five-minute ride to the Island Shangri-La Hotel in Hong Kong's Central District.

Keenan sat quietly, looking out the van window and reminiscing about his former home. It was an amazing place.

The people of Hong Kong had many superstitions but only one religion—making money. Hong Kong's cathedrals were its banks, which towered above the skyline, surrounded by the most expensive real estate on earth. And for all the national wealth, the average local family lived in just five hundred square feet of space, often with parents and grandparents. The city's reputation for high finance and high fashion blended effortlessly with street vendors selling fake Rolexes, costume jade, and cheap suits. The business culture of the city was conducted with ruthless determination and a feverish work ethic held together by a secret network of powerful tycoon family relationships.

Everything about Hong Kong's landscape was vertical. Thousands of high rise-buildings pointed skyward like chopsticks out of the green mountainous terrain surrounded by the South China Sea. Over seven million people packed themselves into an area a hundred times smaller than New York City. The hustle and bustle of Hong Kong was a shock to the senses as crowds of people who were fixated on their mobile phones somehow managed to dodge one another on the city's congested sidewalks. The sweltering summer heat amplified a pungent combination of wet markets, sewer pipes, and a fragrant harbor wafting up from beneath the city streets.

I really miss this place, Keenan thought as they drove out of the Western Harbor Tunnel and into the Central Business District. Glancing at Laura, he saw that she was still sleeping, and he took care not to disturb her.

"We're here, Sir," Gary announced moments later as the van pulled into the entrance of the Island Shangri-La Hotel. The hotel's grand lobby entrance gleamed of white marble contrasted by the hotel's distinguished bellmen dressed in red jackets and red pill hats. It was a popular destination for dignitaries from around the world. Jim was pleased the Agency had given the approval for him to stay there.

Keenan gently leaned over and woke Laura, who was groggy and disoriented from a deep sleep. The van doors opened, and another blast of uncomfortable hot and humid air hit them in the face.

"Welcome to the Shangri-La," the head bellman said, taking the bags from the back of the van. "Please check in, and we'll have your bags sent up to your room right away."

"It will be two rooms," Keenan replied. "Under the names Keenan and Bowman."

"Thank you, sir."

"You don't see service like this at any U.S. hotel," he said to Laura jokingly.

"Clearly we're not in Kansas anymore," she quipped right back, still not entirely sure where she was.

"Thanks for the lift, Gary. We'll see you back here at 10:00 hours."

At the front desk they checked into separate rooms. *What a waste of government money*, Keenan thought as he allowed himself to imagine the possibilities of consolidating to one room with Laura. Even after fifteen hours of flying across the Pacific Ocean she looked beautiful. He caught her glancing a time or two in his direction. Was it his imagination? Or was a connection developing between them? He found it hard to pinpoint anything tangible as evidence, but there was a *feeling*. They shared a unique and coincidental bond, having both lost a parent on 9-11. Laura was slightly shy, but he got the impression she felt relaxed around him—that she genuinely had begun to trust him. And for the first time in Jim's life, he felt an emotional attraction stirring deep inside that he couldn't quite explain. This was different. It wasn't superficial. It wasn't just idle chit chat. This was a woman he barely knew and couldn't stop thinking about.

"Let's meet in the lobby at 1000 hours," Keenan said, trying to get his mind back to business.

"Roger that," Laura replied playfully as she headed over to the coffee station that was set up in the lobby. She filled two cups with coffee and walked back to Keenan who was waiting for an elevator. "Black, right?" she said, handing him a cup.

"Why thank you, Ms. Bowman," Keenan replied with a smile, stepping into the elevator. "See you soon."

Keenan got to his room on the 18th floor. He drank his coffee quickly before heading to the gym for a workout. Vigorous exercise was an effective trick for getting over jet lag. As hard as it could be to muster the enthusiasm to exercise, there was no better way to clear the cobwebs and recharge the batteries. As he panted away on the elliptical machine, he noticed Laura entering the gym, too. She wore Nike running shorts, a halter top, and ASCICS running shoes. She went straight for the treadmill. *That explains the legs,* he thought.

Back in his room, Keenan took a quick shower. While shaving, he found his thoughts again drifting to Laura. His interest was undeniable. But was it unprofessional? She was physically attractive, but he'd dated many attractive women in the past. So, what was it about her? He went through a lengthy list of attributes that he had gathered during their brief time together. She had a great sense of humor, quiet confidence, and a keen intellect all wrapped into a friendly disposition that he found irresistible. *And those legs.*

Laura went back to her room with her thoughts straying repeatedly to Jim. She showered and thought about watching him work out. She had never been able to stay interested in a man for long; most were boring or after only one thing. This man was more than just interesting. She found him intriguing, friendly, but also a little reserved. He was courteous and well-spoken yet down to earth. Not to mention good-looking.

In his room, Keenan dressed in a white button-down shirt, gray trousers, and a blue blazer, then headed down to the hotel lobby at 0955 hours.

Laura was waiting in an Anne Klein fitted blue business dress with matching jacket and black pumps. He detected the slightest hint of perfume. Her hair was styled in a professional updo. She was stunning, and he did a terrible job pretending not to notice. Both felt refreshed and ready to start the day as they climbed into the Consulate van.

"Okay, Gary, let's get going," Keenan said cheerfully.

In the U.S. Consulate meeting room on Garden Road, various Agency and intelligence representatives who had already been briefed on the mission gathered to hear directly from their CIA and FBI visitors on what they had in store for Henry Kwok.

Laura began from her seat. “We’ve got Rothchild on board with the plan. They will arrange for Kwok to travel to New York under the guise of his giving a security presentation to their Board, which meets next week. Before he goes to New York, we plan to surveille him here in Hong Kong to see if he takes us to his Beijing handler,” she continued.

U.S. Consul General Clayton Mattox sat quietly, listening to Bowman while his team took notes and deliberated on the possible pitfalls and consequences. A short, rotund man approaching sixty, Mattox bore a slew of worry lines and an unattractive comb-over. A career State Department official, he was all business, and Hong Kong would be his final assignment before retirement.

“The U.S.-Hong Kong relationship can best be described as *fucked* at the moment,” Mattox said. “The Hong Kong government still hasn’t forgiven us for the Edward Snowden incident way back in 2013. They believe we’re funding the umbrella democracy protests here. And we just imposed sanctions against Hong Kong government officials for enacting a new National Security Law. This morning the Secretary of State imposed direct sanctions on Sarah Ho, Hong Kong’s Chief Executive. I’m not allowed to even speak with her right now.”

“Sir, you can rest assured that we understand the sensitivities here,” James replied. “Our surveillance on Kwok will only be for a few days to see what we can learn. We’re not kidnapping him. His travel to the United States has been carefully orchestrated as a legitimate business trip. Kwok will view his travel to New York as just part of his job”

A brief silence hung over the room.

"Anyone have any questions or concerns for our guests?" Mattox asked. "Speak now or forever hold your peace."

The room remained quiet.

"Okay, then. Good luck to you both; let's get this done. Keep me posted," Mattox ordered in rapid fire. He turned his attention directly to Keenan and Bowman. "Both of you need to understand there is a lot at stake here, including my retirement pension. So don't fuck this up."

"Yes, Sir," Keenan replied for both.

The meeting adjourned, and the attendees scattered to their desks.

Laura leaned over to Keenan as they gathered their notes. "That's the second time in two days we've received those same instructions. I'm starting to take it personally."

Keenan looked into Laura's brilliant green eyes and gave her a sunny grin.

"Let's get going."

SUSPICIONS

CHAPTER 12

It was noon by the time James and Laura left the U.S. Consulate.

"Hungry?" James asked.

"Famished!"

"How about Dim Sum? There's a great place called Yum Cha just down the road," he suggested as he noticed the busy traffic.

"When in Rome..." Laura quipped, adjusting her updo that was starting to droop slightly.

They arrived at the restaurant minutes later, having worked up a bit of sweat in the stifling humidity. They were quickly seated and grateful to beat the traditional Hong Kong lunch hour which began at 12:30.

"So, where do we begin, Mr. Hong Kong?" she asked with a grin as the first round of food was placed on the table.

"Do you know how to use chopsticks?" James asked.

“I mean, where do we begin with Henry Kwok?” she asked in a low voice, deftly picking up her chopsticks and using them as though she had grown up in Chinatown.

James dug into his meal. Between bites he said, “Well, if you want to talk to the masters of the universe in Hong Kong—the billionaire tycoons who really run this city—you go to the Hong Kong Club in Central. Of course, you would need to be a member to get in, and that would take about twenty years given the wait list and secret membership criteria.”

“Sounds like we’re not going to the Hong Kong Club.” She glanced up from her meal with a grin.

“No, we’re not.” After a sip of ice water, James continued. “If you want access to the heavy hitters of international business, then you go to the American Club. I’m still a legacy member there from my parents’ time in Hong Kong. It’s a lot of fun with plenty of old friends to see.”

“So, we start there?” Laura asked after tasting the seasoned rice.

James shook his head. “No, we’re not going there, either. At least not right away. We can go for dinner one night. They have a twenty-five-dollar cheeseburger you have to try.”

Laura’s face brightened. “Okay.”

James grinned. “The fact is, Ms. Bowman, if you really want to know what’s going on in this complicated city, then you go straight to the Members Bar at the Foreign Correspondents Club on Wyndham Street. The locals just call it the FCC. Have you read any of John le Carre's spy novels? *The Spy Who Came in From the Cold*?" he inquired.

"*The Honorable Schoolboy* is my favorite," she replied. "He wrote about the FCC in that one. I didn't realize it was an actual place."

Keenan smiled in appreciation. "We start there," he said. "We'll be looking for a friend of mine. He's like le Carre's *Old Craw* character—the person at the bar who knows everything but looks clueless. The Consulate has a membership card that we can use over there."

"Can't wait," Laura responded and seemed to mean it as she continued to enjoy the lunch.

The final round of dim sum came and went. As the two sat quietly waiting for the check, a wave of exhaustion poured over Laura. It came with nausea and a slight headache.

James could see it in her face. He wasn't feeling much better. "It's the jet lag," he said. "Let's get back to the hotel and rest a bit. We can head out to the FCC around 17:00."

After he paid the check, they took a short taxi ride back to the Shangri-La. As they entered the elevator, they both noticed that "MONDAY" was embroidered into the throw rug on the floor. The hotel changed its elevator floor mats every morning to display the correct day of the week. With so many international travelers dealing with time zone changes, inebriation, and hangovers, this was a welcome feature of the hotel's customer service. The elevator stopped at the eighth floor.

"See you at 17:00," Laura said as she exited to her floor.

"Try not to sleep more than thirty minutes, or you will feel worse," James warned as the elevator doors closed.

★★★

The Foreign Correspondents Club hosted an eclectic mix of journalists, editors, ex-cons, and spies who drank heavily and shared loosely kept secrets. The meal of choice was the chicken pot pie. Displays of award-winning photojournalism adorned the 1980s rustic motif. Oozing of intrigue and well-told stories, it was the perfect place to learn the whereabouts of someone like Henry Kwok. The club's evening Happy Hour started promptly at noon, thanks to club regulars who began with a Bloody Mary brunch.

Keenan and Bowman climbed into a red city taxi for the trip over to Wyndham Street. They entered through the club's brown double doors at 1715 hours. It might as well have been midnight given the level of noise and inebriation displayed by the jovial membership and their guests.

Keenan scanned the room for any familiar faces from his earlier days in Hong Kong—those who might be able to help with the investigation. He hoped his friend would be somewhere in the crowd.

On the far end of the rectangular bar, wearing a red and white checked shirt resembling an Italian restaurant tablecloth, sat Charlie O'Flaherty, a massive man and former rugby star who was now in his late sixties. He had a drinker's red nose and a chipped front tooth that he never bothered to have fixed. A former Hong Kong police officer during the days of British rule, he sat hunched over the bar, leaning into his third gin and tonic. O'Flaherty was a throwback to colonial days and part of a satirical British category known as FILTH—*Failed In London Tried Hong Kong.*

O'Flaherty had somehow ruined his career as a detective in the United Kingdom, though no one really knew the details. The story was it had something to do with the wife of the police chief. Fortunately, he had a family connection in Parliament who was able to get him transferred to the Hong Kong Police Department.

Charlie and his wife Janice lived across the hall from the Keenan family when they were based in Hong Kong. He was a good friend of James's late father, with many a late night spent at the local pubs around Lan Kwai Fung. O'Flaherty had led the sex crimes investigation at the Hong Kong American School and was rumored to have assisted the Triads in getting their revenge inside Stanley Prison. O'Flaherty was exactly the man Keenan was hoping to find. He was Keenan's *Old Craw.*

Jim reflexively grabbed Laura's hand for the short walk over to where his old friend was holding court. "How are you, Charlie?" James asked, waiting for a sign of recognition.

"Jimmy? Is that you?" O'Flaherty squinted as he spoke with a slight slur. "What the fuck are you doing here?"

"Hey Charlie, this is Laura Bowman; she's a colleague of mine from Washington. We're here on special assignment."

Keenan suddenly noticed that he was still holding Laura's hand—and she was still holding his.

O'Flaherty took notice as well. "On assignment, are you, Jimmy?" he asked in a heavy Irish accent. "And how do I get one of those assignments?" he joked with a boisterous laugh.

The hand holding had gone past the point of awkward. Laura let go of Keenan's clasp and reached over to shake O'Flaherty's hand to complete the introduction.

"We're here to gather intel on a former colleague who recently moved to Hong Kong."

"With the company?" Charlie asked, using a popular term for the CIA.

"Formerly with the company," Keenan replied.

"Name?"

"His real name is Henry Kwok, but he could be using an alias," Keenan said, as Laura handed him a photograph.

"Yep. Met him at the bar last Wednesday. Big drinker."

"That means a lot coming from you, Charlie," Keenan joked.

"He said he was on his way to Happy Valley for the horse races. I had to break the news to him that the track closed for the summer because it's too damn hot for the horses to run."

"You spoke with him? Had you seen him here before?"

Charlie thought for a second. "I've seen him in here almost every week, always on a Wednesday. Sits over there at that corner table under the Fall of Saigon photo. Has dinner with the same guy. I thought it strange that he wouldn't know about the horse track being closed. Right after our chat at the bar, he went to the same table and met the same guy for dinner. It occurred to me that he was never intending to go to the horse races. He was just killing time with idle chit chat."

"Can you tell us anything about the guy he meets with?" James pressed.

"He's straight out of Mainland China. Mid-thirties, thin, jet-black hair, and wearing the uniform."

"Uniform?" Laura spoke up.

Charlie burped and nodded. "The Mainland Chinese uniform. We call it China Vuitton. Black suit jacket, mangy white shirt, black suit pants, black shoes, and bright white socks. They must all go to the same thrift shop."

"And you see him most Wednesday nights?" Laura asked.

"Yep. Comes in around 1900 hours. He has a very regular pattern of behavior, Jimmy, for someone who should know better," O'Flaherty said, his police experience coming into play.

James nodded. "That's why he's not working with us anymore, Charlie. Did he say anything else that could be useful?"

O'Flaherty took another sip of his drink before answering. "He said he was living in the Manhattan Apartments in Tai Tam. You should know where that is, Jimmy."

With a wink, James said, "You're the best, Charlie."

Emptying his glass, the older man replied, "Well, then, maybe you could order me another drink as a token of your appreciation?"

James ordered him another gin and tonic. "Can you do me a favor, Charlie? Can you keep an ear open for any information on this guy?"

"No problem," O'Flaherty said in his easygoing manner.

"Laura and I will be here on Wednesday at the bar. It would be good if you didn't know us." "What makes you so sure I'll be here on Wednesday?" O'Flaherty asked with a glint in his eye.

"The same way I know the sun will rise in the east, old friend. Gotta go. We've got work to do."

O'Flaherty reached out and pulled James in close, giving him a burly hug from his barstool. "Your mother Mary, okay?" Charlie murmured.

"Yes, she is, thanks."

"Your dad would be proud of you, Jimmy."

The pair of agents took a red city taxi back to the hotel. It was quiet and slightly awkward between them after the hand-holding incident.

"Meet you in the lobby tomorrow at 07:00," Keenan said as the elevator door opened to the eighth floor, and Laura slowly got out.

"See you then."

They headed to their rooms to update Washington, which was just starting its day on the other side of the world. Laura called Deputy Director Holmes, and Keenan telephoned Tom Fahey.

ZARI

CHAPTER 13

Laura woke up suddenly. She was lying propped on the hotel bed with a yellow legal pad on one side and her laptop on the other. The room lights were still on. Disoriented, she tried to remember where she was. A quick glance at an alarm clock on the nightstand showed a disappointing 03:00.

I need to get back to sleep or tomorrow is going to be pure hell. After a quick visit to the bathroom, she shut off the lights, crawled under the covers, and began tossing and turning to find a comfortable position to fall asleep. It was no use.

Laura had always found the stillness of the early morning a productive time to reflect. She would often go to sleep with an unsolvable problem and then suddenly awaken in the wee hours of the morning with a solution. As she tossed and turned this night, something odd about Henry Kwok came to mind, something she couldn't quite put her finger on. He was clearly selling CIA asset names to the Chinese.

Her thoughts rapidly followed each other: *The notebook we found on him was evidence enough. But could a low-level analyst like Kwok pull this off without help? He needed cover. He needed access. He needed someone to placate CIA internal investigations of his drinking and gambling. Did this guy really work alone?*

Checking again, Laura read 04:00 on the clock, and her thoughts continued to race. She decided she had given enough thought to Kwok for the night and shifted her focus to another suspicious character she had done background work on–CIA Director Charles Wentworth III. *This guy managed to skate through the Senate confirmation hearings in record time without any witnesses being called and with limited testimony. He's a paranoid little man, and he looks like a used car salesman that sleeps in his suits. Not to mention his backward views on women, diversity, and sexual orientation, which are firmly entrenched in the 1950s.*

Wentworth claimed to be a billionaire, but his tax returns had not been included in the Senate vetting process.

Her mind kept churning. She made mental notes on how to follow up on her suspicions before her thoughts turned comfortably to James Francis Keenan. *He's a serious sort. But handsome with an adorable smile and a great sense of humor. A jock with a fighter pilot's ego. But not in an arrogant way. Why is a guy like this not married or divorced? What fatal flaw am I going to discover beneath the surface?*

She decided to focus on his smile and finally drifted off to sleep at 04:30. Her alarm sounded promptly at 05:00.

After swimming laps in the hotel pool and a room service breakfast of coffee, yogurt, and fruit, Laura grabbed her Nikon P900 telephoto camera and headed to the lobby at 07:00. The elevator throw rug now read "TUESDAY."

James quickly spotted her. "Did you get some sleep?"

"Yes. And laps in the pool to wake up. I'm ready to go." She gave him a warm smile.

Gary Lau waited outside in a beige civilian Toyota Alphard van with private license plates. Toyota vans were ubiquitous across Hong Kong. They included curtains on the windows that could be drawn without looking suspicious.

Outside, the summer air was again hot and thick with humidity. Sunshine beat down on the pavement, which was damp from a late-night rain, resulting in a layer of steam hovering just above the ground.

"Gary, let's go to Tai Tam first. We want a spot right outside the Manhattan Apartment Building where the taxi stand is."

"Got it, Sir." The van departed for the forty-minute ride to the back side of the island.

"Did you sleep, Jim?" Laura asked. She suddenly realized that she had been calling her colleague "Jim" as the informal nickname for James. Apparently, he didn't mind.

Stifling a yawn, he said, "I did some reading and took half an Ambien. That got me through to 03:00. Then I watched a cricket sporting match from India on television, which put me to sleep quickly," he joked. "Had a good workout this morning, though. If I had known you were swimming laps, I would have sneaked in to cheer you on," he quipped.

"Swimming and running keep me sane."

"Swimming for me is more like controlled drowning. I've never been able to get the hang of it," James replied, shaking his head.

"You need a good coach," Laura suggested.

"Are you volunteering?" he asked with a raised eyebrow.

"We'll see."

The van arrived at the Manhattan Apartment Complex on 33 Tai Tam Road and pulled into one of the open parking spaces facing the taxi stand. The Manhattan was a popular location for international families living in Hong Kong. It was made up of four high-rise apartment buildings with an Olympic-size swimming pool and tennis courts.

Laura set up her camera and pulled the curtain across the window so that just the lens was exposed.

"This is where we lived when my dad was based here," Keenan said thoughtfully. "We spent a lot of time at the American Club which is right there," he said pointing across the street. "This area is full of memories."

She glanced around. "It must have been fun."

"It was. My old school is just down the road. That was great, too—before they turned it into a house of horrors." He didn't go into it any further, and Laura didn't ask.

A line was starting to form at the taxi stand.

"Kwok should be out soon," Keenan noted.

"There!" Laura said as Henry Kwok exited the Manhattan's iron gate and got in line. She began snapping photos as one by one the taxis picked up passengers.

"Okay, Gary, our guy is next for a ride. We follow his taxi."

"Yes, Sir."

Kwok got in a red taxi and headed off to Central with Keenan and Bowman following two car lengths behind.

"Let's see if he stops anywhere before going to the Rothchild office, Gary."

"Got it."

The taxi went directly to Hong Kong's Central District and dropped Kwok off at the front entrance to the Rothchild Auction House on Chater Road.

Laura hurriedly kept snapping photos, trying for the best angles and lighting.

Kwok walked straight into the building.

"Okay, let's find a place to park where we can keep an eye on the entrance and see when he comes out."

They circled to the other side of Chater Road and parked at a ninety-degree angle to the front doors.

"Now we wait," Keenan said, leaning back.

"I hate waiting," Laura said.

"Gary, do you have any music up there you can play? Agent Bowman is already bored with our company," Keenan joked.

"Very funny." She elbowed his side.

★★★

At 12:32 Henry Kwok walked out the office building door.

"See him?"

"Yes, Sir, I have him."

"He's not getting a taxi. He must be walking to get some lunch," Laura said, snapping more photos.

Kwok headed next door to a noodle shop called Chen's on Chater.

"Can you back us up and get us in front of that restaurant?"

Kwok was seated al fresco and chose an umbrella table in the restaurant's open courtyard. The van was in a perfect location for surveillance.

"Nice work, Gary," Laura commented with the camera telephoto lens now fixed squarely on Kwok. "How can you eat outside on a sweltering day like today?" she asked, unconsciously pushing a stray lock of hair into her low ponytail.

At 12:40, a tall Middle Eastern woman named Zari dressed in a white blouse and a pink chiffon hijab headscarf arrived at the noodle shop and sat down at Kwok's table.

"This is interesting," Laura said, zooming in on the woman's face.

As she snapped more pictures, Keenan set up an UZI OD-1 listening device and aimed its sound collection disk directly at Kwok's table. "Shit. This thing is only good to about 300 feet. All I'm getting is background noise."

★★★

Henry Kwok knew his Beijing handler only by his code name, Panda. His instructions from Panda at the FCC the week before had been specific. "Go to Chen's Noodle Restaurant on Tuesday at 12:30. Get a table outdoors. An Iraqi woman in a pink hajib with a backpack will approach your table and ask if the dumplings are as good as people say. Your reply will be that the pork buns are especially good, and then you will invite her to sit down. She will verbally give you vital information. Do not write anything down. She will hand you a data key. You are not to look at its contents. We will meet back here at the FCC for dinner next Wednesday. You will tell me in detail what she said and hand me the data key. Is that clear?"

"Yes."

"Do you have any questions?"

"No."

And with that, the meeting with Zari had been set.

★★★

Zari knew her spy craft. She had taken three taxis and a public yellow bus around the city and changed outfits twice in hotel lobby bathrooms to shake off anyone who might have tried to follow her. The swath of her hajib exposed a beautifully contoured face. Kwok guessed she was about thirty years old. She had dark eyes, perfectly sculpted eyebrows, and glowing olive skin. Zari's looks were deceptive. She was a seasoned Iraqi intelligence officer from the group known as Al Sukuor, a secretive unit used to penetrate Al-Qaeda cells by posing as Islamic Jihadists. It was dangerous work but highly effective in cracking Al-Qaeda's strategy, tactics, and terrorist targets.

Zari asked about the dumplings and was satisfied with Kwok's correct response. She sat down and looked at him in silence, sizing him up before she began speaking in a low voice.

"We have evidence from our agents inside an Al-Qaeda cell that a major terrorist attack on the United States is imminent," she said. "We've learned that these attacks will use nuclear weapons."

Kwok listened and tried to imagine nukes dropped from an airplane over the United States.

"You must get this information to the Ministry of State Security in Beijing as soon as possible."

"I don't understand," Kwok replied. "Why are you giving this information to us instead of directly to the Americans?"

There was a pause, and against Zari's better judgment, she went on to explain. "My government in Iraq would like China to rebuild our devastated infrastructure, and we are asking that China pay for these projects as well," Zari added.

Kwok interjected, "I still don't understand. How does this information help us in Beijing?"

Zari continued, "My government is giving you this information as a supreme gesture of goodwill, which will allow your government to reset its deteriorating relationship with the United States. If we allow your leaders in Beijing to take credit for informing the Americans of this plot, and America avoids a devastating nuclear attack, it will change hearts and minds. It will shift the calculus of your relationship with the United States overnight and establish an unprecedented level of trust between your two countries. You will be able to continue your rise on the world stage uninterrupted, and in return, we ask that your government build the roads, bridges, power plants, and digital infrastructure that we so desperately need." Zari suddenly stopped, fearing she had said too much.

She reached across the table and handed Kwok a small data storage key containing critical information about the planned attack, including details on target locations and delivery methods.

"I cannot tell you what is on this data storage device, and you are not to look at it. Is that clear?"

"I understand—those are my orders as well." He gave her an agreeable smile.

From the van across the street, Laura snapped photos of the storage key changing hands.

"Please get this to Panda as soon as possible," Zari said anxiously. "The data key is password protected, and we've already texted the access code to the proper person at your Ministry of State Security." She got up from the table. "Good luck to you," she said, heading for the street.

Kwok pocketed the data key and ordered lunch.

"Let's get back to the Consulate, Gary," Keenan directed.

When Kwok returned to work, he was summoned to the office of the Chief Operating Officer, Neil Hoyt. A chubby, flamboyant Brit wearing a neon blue suit with a yellow tie, Hoyt had been in Hong Kong with Rothchild since 2003.

"Good afternoon, Neil," Kwok said after tapping lightly on the office door. "You wanted to see me?"

Neil glanced up and smiled. "Henry. How are you? Please sit down."

"We need you to go to our head office in New York next week and give a presentation to our Board on the work you're doing with cybersecurity. My assistant Brenda will take care of your flight itinerary and hotel. Put an overview draft presentation together, and let me see a copy before you head out."

"Will do, Neil. Thanks."

Kwok returned to his desk thinking about his lunch meeting. He replayed the conversation again in his head, and despite Panda's instructions, he took some notes for his upcoming meeting at the FCC. He placed the data key in a zipped pocket inside his computer bag. The gravity of Zari's words began to sink in. Since he would now be traveling to the United States himself, her concern about an imminent nuclear attack weighed on him.

PANDA

CHAPTER 14

Back at the U.S. Consulate, Jim and Laura greeted Clayton Mattox in a secure room adjoining his office.

"Sir, we got a good look at Kwok earlier today," Keenan said to Mattox, who listened attentively. "He met with a Middle Eastern woman for lunch. There was an exchange of a data storage key. We've sent the photos back to Langley for facial recognition and analysis."

"What's that about? She can't be his handler!" Mattox exclaimed.

James clarified, "No, she's not Kwok's handler. But the data key he was given today should take us to his handler. We believe he will attempt some kind of handoff tomorrow evening."

There was a brief pause by Mattox. "And how will that happen?"

"Sir, it's best you don't know. We wanted to update you that things are going to plan, and Laura and I should be out of your way in a few days."

Mattox grunted. "Let's hope so. And what about Kwok's trip to the U.S.?"

James glanced at Laura to see if she wanted to jump in. Her smiled encouraged him to continue. "Rothchild will be informing Kwok this afternoon about his business flight to New York. We don't anticipate any issues."

"Well, then, thank you both for the update. Now if you'll excuse me." The meeting ended abruptly as Mattox returned to an American Chamber of Commerce briefing that was already in progress.

★★★

On Wednesday morning the sky turned ominous with dark clouds, torrential rain, and dangerous lightning. The rain fell faster than Hong Kong could absorb it, as waterfalls formed on the mountainous landscape, flooding the streets below.

James and Laura followed the same morning routine, tracking Henry Kwok from his apartment in Tai Tam to his office in Central as the rain pelted their windshield. This morning there was nothing remarkable in Kwok's behavior. The real objective would be that evening at the FCC where hopefully Kwok would be meeting with his Beijing handler.

With the van parked, Gary went to get everyone coffees from the nearby Starbucks, and Laura took the opportunity of being alone with Keenan to speak to him confidentially. "Jim, I've been wondering about a few things," she said as they sat alone in the van.

"Shoot," Jim said.

"Does it seem possible to you that a low-level guy like Henry Kwok could pull off what he did inside the Agency without any higher-level assistance? It seems a stretch that he would be able to obtain the PROJECT LUCY asset names along with all the other information he stole without any help. And how did he manage to keep getting past his internal probation? My files show he should have been fired at least two years ago. Who kept letting him slide?"

James absorbed her words.

"You've been giving this some thought." He shot her an admiring glance.

"I didn't have much to do between 03:00 and 05:00 staring at the hotel ceiling," she replied.

James sighed. "I hired Kwok. He seemed like a bright guy, fluent in Mandarin. Good intelligence skills. Then he started to slip."

"So why didn't he get let go earlier?" Laura gave him a penetrating look.

"I put in for his termination twice through the chain of command. Both times it went through Tom. The last time I submitted the termination request Wentworth decided to extend his probation period again instead of firing him. At least that's what Tom told me. I never heard directly from Wentworth. Tom told me that Kwok was running a sensitive operation involving a Chinese billionaire in New York and that he needed to stay on for a while longer."

Laura shook her head. "Didn't that seem questionable to you?"

"It seemed odd, but not unprecedented," Keenan said. "We're not supposed to do domestic operations in the United States. That's your purview over at the FBI. I figured if Kwok was being used for a special assignment in New York it must be important to management, so I left it alone."

With a searching look, Laura continued, "Well, you bring up my next question, Jim. What do we know about Charles Wentworth III other than he's raised millions of dollars for the Republican Party?"

Jim asked, "What do you mean?"

Settling more comfortably in her seat, Laura said, "I've read everything there is to read on Wentworth's confirmation. It's the worst vetting process I've ever seen. He skated through the Senate, which barely asked him anything beyond his name and address. His business dealings have been sketchy, to say the least. Wentworth never had to produce his tax returns as part of the confirmation process, so nobody knows what he's worth."

Jim stretched and looked out the van window to see if Gary was returning yet. "You really think Wentworth is a problem?"

"I don't know." She shrugged. "He just seems creepy and secretive."

James smirked. "We deal a lot with 'creepy and secretive' at CIA, Laura. And so do you at the FBI."

"Wentworth did submit a financial disclosure statement to the Senate. But he never consented to a qualified blind trust," Laura continued.

"That's not unusual as long as the Office of Government Ethics clears his portfolio of any conflicts in advance," James replied.

"Did you know a sizable portion of Wentworth's investment portfolio is in Chinese technology companies?" she asked.

"Really?" James asked.

"Did you also know that Wentworth was a non-executive board member of Huawei in China?" she added.

"I didn't know that," Keenan said with a raised brow as Gary returned to the van with the coffees. "It just seems strange," Laura said, shaking her head.

★★★

Henry Kwok worked on his Rothchild board presentation from morning straight through to 17:00 before taking a taxi to his apartment to clean up before dinner. He was eager to meet with Panda that evening to share the news about the Al-Qaeda attack. He didn't want any nukes going off in New York City while he was visiting. He climbed into a taxi, unaware that the air conditioning was broken. With the windows rolled down, he loosened his tie and fanned his face with a newspaper.

Laura decided her iPhone would be the best way to take pictures inside the Club, and James agreed. They sat in the van across from his apartment building wearing baseball hats and sunglasses, hoping Kwok would emerge. At 18:30 he came walking out to the taxi stand.

"We're on," Laura said.

"If he is meeting with his handler, he will use diversion maneuvers to shake any tails," Keenan said as they followed Kwok's taxi back toward Central. During the drive, Keenan thought about Laura's suspicions regarding Charles Wentworth III.

As the taxi reached Central, it didn't go to the Foreign Correspondents Club. Instead, it pulled up at the front entrance of the Mandarin Oriental Hotel.

"Pull in behind him, Gary," Keenan instructed. "You stay in the van," he said to Laura, "and I'll follow him into the hotel. Stay on the phone with me, and I'll tell you what to do next," he said, dialing her number and putting in his ear pods. "Good?"

"Got it."

Keenan jumped out of the van, pulling his baseball hat over his head. He followed Kwok into the main entrance of the hotel. Kwok walked straight through the white marble lobby to the hotel's back entrance on Connaught Road.

"He's in diversion mode," Keenan told Laura over the phone. "He's going out the rear of the hotel. Tell Gary to drive around onto Connaught Road."

As the van sped around back, Kwok hailed another taxi and got in.

Keenan jumped back in the van as it came around the corner. "Keep on him."

"Got him," Gary said, intently navigating traffic.

"Well, it looks like we have our answer. He's definitely meeting his handler," Jim said confidently. They arrived at the FCC a few minutes later.

"Okay, I'm ready," Laura said, opening the van door.

"I need to stay in the van, so he doesn't recognize me," Keenan said. "Text me what's happening from inside."

Bowman walked in and chose the seat at the bar which had the best view to Kwok's table. She ordered a drink and struggled to recall the Consulate's membership number so she could pay for it. Charlie O'Flaherty was sitting directly across the bar, pretending not to notice her.

Kwok entered the bar holding a copy of *The South China Morning Post*. Taking a seat, he placed the folded newspaper on the table and began studying the menu. Moments later, he was joined by a lanky Chinese man wearing the China Vuitton uniform—exactly as Charlie O'Flaherty had described him.

Panda was a career intelligence officer with China's MSS—Ministry of State Security. He had been responsible for recruiting Henry Kwok and gave him the codename 'Firefly.'

"Did you get the data key?" Panda asked in Mandarin, lifting his menu close to his face as if reading the small print.

"All according to plan," Kwok replied in Mandarin. "It's in my newspaper."

"Did she tell you anything?" Panda asked without looking up.

"She said a terrorist attack by Al-Qaeda on the United States is imminent and that the data key I'm giving you is urgent and must get to Beijing. She also said the access code to open the file has already been sent to MSS." He shot a questioning glance at the man across the table.

"Yes, we have it."

"She told me that the attack would use nuclear weapons."

"Anything else?" Panda inquired.

"Yes. She said Iraq is asking for our help in return. To rebuild their country."

"And they will get our help," Panda said as he stood up from the table.

Bowman pretended to do a facetime call from her seat at the bar, holding her iPhone up and talking aloud while taking pictures of the two men.

Panda casually picked up the newspaper containing the data key and headed to the door.

"Gotcha," Bowman whispered as she photographed the handoff.

"We've got him," Laura texted to the van. "I'm coming out."

The van approached the FCC and Bowman got in.

"It's time to get this asshole back to the States, so we can find out what's going on here," Keenan said.

"You got that right," Laura said, reviewing the photos she'd taken in the club.

They now had enough probable cause to arrest Henry Kwok on suspicion of espionage when he landed at JFK in New York.

"How about we refreshen up and go out for a proper dinner?" Keenan asked.

"That sounds great, Jim. We earned it," Laura replied with a smile as Gary turned the van around and headed back toward the Shangri-La hotel.

ROOM 814

CHAPTER 15

Keenan was first to arrive at the popular Lobster Bar behind the hotel's main lobby. He wore jeans and an untucked white button-down shirt with rolled up sleeves.

He stood at the bar with one foot on the brass step rail and the other planted firmly on the floor and slowly panned the eclectic mix of patrons. Businesspeople, mostly. A few high-end working girls from Russia were chatting up potential clients twice their age.

The bartender, a tall, slender man wearing a black vest, white shirt, and bowtie, approached. "Good evening," he said with a British accent. "My name is Trevor. I will be your mixologist this evening."

Oh shit, a mixologist! Keenan thought. *It will take him fifteen minutes to make a drink that should only take thirty seconds. At double the price.*

"Something to drink?" Trevor asked.

"Do you have Don Julio tequila?"

"Of course, Sir."

"I'd like a Don Julio margarita, no salt. And Trevor, make it a double please."

"Of course, Sir."

With the day's adrenaline wearing off, James was tired and a little nervous as he waited for Laura to arrive. He held the seat next to him open for her. The days had been hectic but contained a highly successful mission overall. Tom Fahey in Washington had been updated on their progress, and James looked forward to rehashing the mission with Laura over a drink and dinner.

Trevor the mixologist eventually showed up with a refreshing double margarita—just what the doctor ordered.

James took a healthy swig to help quiet the butterflies in his stomach. *Why am I so damn nervous?* His anticipation of Laura's arrival intensified as he glanced at his watch for the third time. She was late. Or maybe she had fallen asleep.

The bartender came over again, noticing that James was waiting for someone. "I guess the price you pay for punctuality is loneliness," he said humorously. "I am sure your guest will arrive soon," he said.

"Thank you," James said dryly, wondering why the bartender would know that.

A moment later she entered the Lobster Bar through the main doors, wearing a simple blue and white sleeveless sundress and coordinating white heels. The dress accentuated her sleek figure and shoulder-length hair; a simple gold pendant adorned her neck. Laura looked refreshed and energized as she spotted James and made her way over to the bar.

Wow, Keenan thought, thankful that the initial swig of his margarita had finally kicked in. "You clean up well, Agent Bowman," he said as she approached.

"And who would have guessed that you own a pair of jeans, Agent Keenan?" she teased, taking the seat beside him.

"What would you like to drink? We need to order now, so it will arrive before Christmas," James joked.

"What kind of margarita is that?" she asked, pointing.

"Don Julio."

"What can I get for you, Ms. Bowman?" Trevor asked, leaning slightly over the bar.

"How do you know the bartender?" James inquired.

Laura gave James a mock superior look. "He's not a bartender, Jim. He's a mixologist. And a woman never tells her secrets. I'll have a Bombay Sapphire martini, painfully dry—with a twist."

James gave a nod of respect to Laura's drink order.

When her drink arrived, they toasted, being careful not to spill. Trevor politely waited a moment and then asked if they would care to move to the table in the corner.

James saw that the table would provide welcome privacy and looked at Laura to see if she agreed.

"It's okay with me, Jim. I arranged it with Trevor an hour ago."

They got up and went to the small round table with a starched white tablecloth. A vase of fresh flowers and an intimate votive candle added to the romantic mood. They sat across from one another.

"You did great work on this mission, Laura."

"It's been a pleasure working with you, Jim, and getting to see the place where you grew up," she replied, toasting glasses.

Their discussion focused first on their work and the unfortunate story of Henry Kwok. All the while the drinks kept flowing as the chemistry between the pair blossomed. The ambiance of the cozy corner table facilitating the mood, just as Laura had intended.

"So, what made you become an FBI agent?" James asked with genuine interest.

Laura sipped her drink before answering. "Well, I come from a long line of firefighters. My dad, Greg Bowman, was Battalion Chief with the New York Fire Department, third generation. I was the only girl in the family, and my dad wanted me to be a career woman. So, my parents sent me to Simmons College in Boston. I majored in accounting. But all I ever really wanted to be was a firefighter like my dad."

"Really?" James pictured how attractive she would look in a firefighter's helmet.

"I wanted to be part of that firehouse fraternity my dad raised me in. It's a community that only firefighters know. I wanted to be a hero like he was, running into burning buildings when everyone else was running out. He had a wonderful soft side to him. He loved greeting the kids who visited the station on field trips, letting them climb all over the firetrucks. He used to take me to all his softball games against the other fire stations. I held his bat and glove on the sidelines. He even had a team jersey made with my name on the back. I never wanted to take it off."

Jim nodded empathetically. "And on 9-11, wasn't it his battalion that was first into the World Trade Center?" he asked, trying not to show the emotion that had welled up in his eyes from hearing Laura's memories.

"Yeah. That Tuesday morning, he went to Ground Zero with fourteen of his men. Those guys were like brothers and uncles to me. None of them were ever found. I still get angry for not being able to say goodbye. Nothing to bury. No real closure."

James shook his head. "I'm sorry, Laura. I shouldn't have brought it up."

She lowered her voice as if to make sure no one else could hear. "I still talk to my dad all the time. Sometimes early in the morning when I'm lying awake in the quiet, I can feel his gentle presence telling me that everything will be okay."

"Are you not okay?" James asked, concerned.

She raised her eyes to meet his. "I'm damn good at my job, Jim. But to be honest, my attempts at relationships have mostly ended in disaster. I'm not fair to the poor buggers who ask me out on dates. I hold them to unrealistic standards. I want them to be as special as my father was, but I know they never will be. My work keeps me motivated—it gives me purpose. But it always feels like there is a gaping black hole in my life when it comes to companionship. Something is missing. Nobody wants to be alone.

So maybe someday I'll meet someone who is right for me. I think that's what my dad is trying to tell me. That I will be okay and that I'll meet a man one of these days who sweeps me off my feet and who isn't intimidated by my job."

A brief silence fell between them, and Keenan took a sip of his margarita, looking into her radiant green eyes.

"After 9-11," Laura continued, "the Firehouse paid for my education. All of it. Tuition, room and board, spending money. They have been like family to my mother and me. I wanted to make a difference with my life to show them my appreciation, and decided that service in the FBI would be a worthwhile career to help fight the bad guys. I also found firing a Barretta pistol to be quite liberating."

"Good to know," Keenan quipped.

Laura flexed her shoulders to increase circulation after sitting so long.

"And you, Mr. Hong Kong, what's your story? I googled you, by the way," she admitted with a giggle.

The drinks kept flowing as Trevor brought over another round.

"Not much to tell," James began. "My father was an executive at State Street Bank in Boston. He was full of life, too. Loved sports. Loved to travel. He leaped at the opportunity to take the family to Hong Kong when State Street needed an executive in Asia. Most of my childhood experience was in this amazing city. I kissed my first girlfriend on Stanley Beach near here. And you will find this interesting—my parents made me attend Cotillion."

"You were in Cotillion?" Laura interjected with a laugh. "I can't picture you sitting through a class in table etiquette with your little suit and tie, Jim."

"Yeah, it was painful," he admitted. "But I know which fork to use at social events, and I notice most of my colleagues wait to see which utensil I pick before they reach for theirs."

"Too funny." She smiled graciously.

"When the family moved back to the States, my father sent me to Milton Academy boarding school. It was a great experience. My favorite subject was history, especially American history. My roommate and I started an American History Club at Milton, which is still active today."

"Interesting. What about sports?"

"I played football and ice hockey. Not the kind of sports you can play for a lifetime, so I learned to play golf and tennis as well. After Milton, it was off to the Naval Academy and then to fly jets."

"And 9-11?" She leaned in closer with her cheek on her hand to hear his reply.

"I was watching the live news report on television with my friends that morning when my dad's plane out of Boston hit the South Tower. But I didn't know he was on the flight until my mother called the school."

"That's horrible!" Her eyes widened.

"I decided I was going to join the military and make sure no kid would ever have to witness what I did that day. When my flying days were over in the Navy, the CIA seemed like a perfect fit. Tom Fahey was a big reason why I joined. He's been like a father to me, a real mentor. Working for him has been the experience of a lifetime."

"I don't know him that well, Jim, but he seems like a gentleman—intelligent and down to earth. He clearly looks at you with pride, given all you've been able to accomplish."

"He reminds me of my father in many ways. If I ever have kids of my own, I'll make sure they spend time with Tom, so they can get an idea of what their grandfather was like."

"You miss him," Laura said with tears welling up in her eyes.

"Every day. I just hope he's proud of me."

"I'm sure he is," she said softly.

As the conversation continued, their legs and knees touched under the table in playful flirtation. There finally came a point where they ran out of words. They sipped the last of their cocktails and just gazed at each other. They had shared their most intimate stories, revealing more than either thought possible. Maybe it was the drinks, but each recognized there was much more happening between them.

"I realize this is unprofessional, but would you mind if I kissed you?" James politely asked as he leaned in closer to Laura.

She smiled and gave him a gentle kiss on the lips. Again, they found themselves staring at each other in silence.

"You have incredible blue eyes, Mr. Keenan," Laura whispered.

"My mother used to call them bedroom eyes," he confessed.

"I can certainly see why, Mr. Keenan," she whispered, her face full of tenderness.

She leaned in closer and put her lips up to James's ear, gently placing her hand on top of his. "I'm in room 814. Why don't you give me a few minutes and then come up?"

She picked up her purse from the table and headed out toward the elevator. Her perfect figure looked as beautiful and inviting on departure as it had on her arrival.

After giving Laura a reasonable lead, James headed to the elevator, mentally running through the pros and cons of what was about to happen. Laura had admitted to being unlucky in love, and he had not done much better. He wondered if this was a disaster in the making. Twice he stopped in the hallway while walking to Room 814. Twice he considered turning back. But this didn't feel like another one-night fling. He knew that feeling all too well. He had never felt this way about any woman before. They had already shared so much of their past with each other, and a close connection had formed. Something kept his legs moving in Laura's direction while his brain continued to rationalize the journey.

He gently knocked on the door.

Laura opened it slowly, drawing James into the room. She was barefoot and noticeably shorter without heels. The soft sound of chamber music played from a Bose speaker clock next to the bed. Two lamps on the far side of the room were the only illumination, except for the city lights that twinkled through a large window. As the door closed, the two embraced in a passionate kiss.

In an instant, all common sense and Agency protocol vanished. There would be no turning back.

Their movements were at first awkward and clumsy as they struggled to find each other's buttons and zippers, shuffling haphazardly toward the king-size bed. With his jeans on the floor, James slowly held Laura's hair to one side as he unzipped her sun dress. The zipper ran the full length of her garment, exposing her smooth, tanned back. The dress slid off her shoulders and fell to the floor.

Taking a seat on the bed, Laura lay back with arms raised over her head.

"Incredible," James murmured as he gazed at her beauty from above.

The intensity of James's touch, his awareness of where to touch, and the tenderness of his lips covering every part of her body sent Laura to a level of arousal and intimacy she had never experienced.

She decided it was her turn to take control, rolling James over to lie face up on the bed. She listened to him gasp with pleasure as she slowly explored every inch of his athletic build. Her sensitive touch, erotic gyrations, and playful experimentation took him by surprise. They stirred each other's passions in an intimate marathon of ecstasy and recovery until neither had the energy to continue.

Rolling over in exhaustion, they stared at the ceiling in silence.

"Ooops!" Laura finally said jokingly as they nestled in each other's arms. They had a good laugh before exchanging the kind of pillow talk lovers often share.

James finally got up and waded through the discarded clothing strewn across the floor before reaching the mini bar. He opened two bottles of water and brought them over to the bed to quench their thirst.

Finishing his drink quickly, James got up and started looking for his clothes.

Laura hit him with a pillow. "You're welcome to stay, you know."

"I'm calling room service. Pizza okay with you?"

"Ah…pizza!"

He placed the order by phone and then took out the two oversized terry cloth bathrobes hanging in the hallway closet. He put one robe on and handed the other to Laura. They briefly dozed in each other's arms until room service interrupted thirty minutes later.

Eating from the coffee table, they quietly watched CNN before crawling back into bed. The digital clock read 1:03. James set a wakeup call for 06:00, which would give them plenty of time to make their flight to New York.

Laura reached over and hit the master switch on the panel beside the bed. The room went dark, and the couple fell into a deep slumber, clumsily entwined in each other's bathrobes.

RETURN

CHAPTER 16

James and Laura were startled out of a deep sleep by the hotel's early-morning wakeup call. They lay face up, staring at the bedroom ceiling, quietly filling in the memory gaps from the night before and awkwardly contemplating what to do next.

A moment later, the pair rolled out of bed and scrambled to get organized, sifting through hastily discarded clothing strewn across the floor. Laura tossed her things onto a nearby chair while James began dressing.

"Lobby at 08:00?" James asked softly, pulling on his jeans.

"Sure," Laura said, smiling as she checked her cell phone messages and headed for the shower, her body barely visible inside her large robe.

James gave her a kiss on the cheek and returned to his room on the 18th floor. He decided on a quick workout to make the upcoming trip more bearable.

Postponing her shower, Laura crawled back into bed to reminisce about the previous night. Catching a wispy scent of James's cologne on her pillow, she took a deep sniff and smiled, replaying the evening in her mind. Moments later, glancing at the clock, she saw it was time to pack.

On schedule, they each made their way down to the lobby and checked out of the hotel. Gary waited patiently near the front doors.

It was going to be a long day: a grueling flight to New York followed by a myriad of details to be worked out in preparation for the arrival and arrest of Henry Kwok. Keenan and Bowman sat quietly during the ride out to the airport, each anticipating the mission ahead.

Laura gazed out her window at the high-rise buildings and the bustle of morning rush hour. She now understood Jim's love affair with Hong Kong. *Could he ever fall in love with me?* she wondered.

James grappled with a range of fluttery emotions. One-night stands were his modus operandi. Easy to manage. No commitments. Just sex. But Laura was different. She stirred intense feelings in him. Yet, the situation scared him. Serious relationships lead to ugly break ups. He was keenly aware of his track record for failed relationships and losing the people he cared most deeply about.

As they approached the departure terminal, James looked over and saw that Laura had dozed off. He gently nudged her as the van came to a stop.

"I was having a wonderful dream about last night," she murmured with a mischievous smile, opening her eyes.

"You'll have plenty of time to pick up where you left off over the next fifteen hours," James replied tenderly.

“I don’t think I could survive fifteen hours of a dream like that,” she said with a whisper. “But I’m willing to try.”

James laughed and opened the van door as Gary gave a suspicious glance in the rearview mirror. “Sir, the United check-in counter is on aisle D in the main terminal. Have a safe flight.”

“Thanks, Gary. You’ve been a great help,” James said, stepping out onto the curb.

★★★

As they sat in the United Airlines lounge awaiting their flight, Laura picked up a copy of *The Economist* from the magazine rack and began reading the cover story entitled “Huawei and the Rise of China Inc.”

“What exactly is China’s endgame, Jim? What are they trying to achieve with all the blustering and chest thumping?” Laura asked in a low voice, pointing to the magazine cover.

A pretty intense question to be asking someone with a hangover, Keenan thought with amusement.

“It’s simple,” he replied. “China wants to restore their historical place in the world as the preeminent superpower. They want to dominate high tech markets using the intellectual property they steal from us in the United States, and they want to convert the world over to their autocratic one-party system of government. Oh, and they want to take back Taiwan by whatever means possible,” James explained.

"And do you think Huawei is really working for the Chinese government?" she asked.

"Huawei is the Chinese government," Keenan said with emotion as he pointed back at the magazine cover.

"And what would it take to become a board member of a Chinese company like Huawei?" she asked.

"You would need to be very wealthy and connected, and you would need to offer Huawei some kind of influence that money couldn't buy," Jim replied.

"So, Charles Wentworth wasn't asked to be a member of Huawei's board of directors because of his personality and his badly wrinkled suits?" she inquired smartly.

Jim gave her a thoughtful glance, acknowledging that she had made her point, but he was unwilling to take the conversation further.

"Time to board," he said, standing and grabbing their carry-on bags.

"I'm ready," she said, taking a last sip of coffee and putting the magazine back on the rack.

Jim handed her an Ambien tablet. "Take half after dinner. It will get you back to that dream of yours," he said with grin. She accepted the sleeping pill without fanfare as her mind continued to churn over the many questions surrounding Charles Wentworth III.

★★★

At 1800 hours that evening, Henry Kwok boarded Cathay Pacific flight 888 nonstop service to JFK International

Airport. He located seat 12B in the business class cabin and settled in for a long flight. It would be his first trip to New York City in more than a decade and the last time he would ever see Hong Kong.

SCHEMES

CHAPTER 17

Zhongnanhai, Central Headquarters of the Communist Party • Beijing

China's Premier Li Wan was popular among Beijing's senior leadership. A heavyset man with jet black hair courtesy of bimonthly dye treatments, he looked younger than his sixty years. As he walked down the long main hallway of the Zhongnanhai government compound, he wondered about the hastily called meeting by his friend General Gao Zheng, head of China's powerful Ministry of State Security, also known as the Guoanbu.

General Gao sat awaiting Li's arrival. He was similar in girth and hairstyle to Li but with gaunt facial features exposing the burden of a million State secrets and a five-pack-a-day smoking habit.

"My old friend," the Premier said as he entered the small receiving area to shake Gao's hand. He motioned for Gao to accompany him to the secure meeting room he had arranged and to have a seat in one of the four leather chairs that surrounded a coffee table. The doors were closed by Li's personal secretary who remained in the room to take notes.

"General, the MSS did an exemplary job in exposing the CIA's PROJECT LUCY operation. I want to commend you on behalf of President Jiang. He appreciates your efforts in having these traitors executed so swiftly. Makes people think twice before betraying their country."

"Thank you, Premier," Gao replied, maintaining respect of title despite their close friendship.

"Let me also extend my congratulations on turning the American, Henry Kwok, over to our side."

"His code name is Firefly," Gao quickly interjected.

"Yes, Firefly. Forgive me, I shouldn't have used his real name."

"Sir, the intelligence we have been gathering from Firefly's defection is extraordinary, and the timing could not be better," Gao said. "That's why I needed to speak to you today privately."

Premier Li motioned for his secretary to leave the meeting room. She closed the door quietly behind her.

"What's going on?" the Premier inquired, leaning in toward his friend with a look of concern.

Gao shifted in his chair, unsure of how to begin. He took a sip of tea from the glass in front of him to clear his throat. "The Iraqi intelligence service contacted us last week requesting a meeting in Beijing. We thought this was too risky and arranged to have them meet with Firefly in Hong Kong as a first step. That meeting has now taken place."

"And what have we learned?"

"Iraqi intelligence has uncovered a plot for a massive terrorist attack by Al-Qaeda against the United States that looks to be imminent. We believe the intelligence is credible. There is information on a data key that is highly specific on how they plan to execute the attack," Gao explained, adding, "Al-Qaeda plans to use nuclear weapons."

"Nuclear weapons?"

"We can't confirm where Al-Qaeda got the nuclear weapons; we suspect Iran or Pakistan, but we know they will be deployed aboard two cargo ships heading for the United States. One is going to Los Angeles, and the other is heading to the U.S. East Coast via the Panama Canal. It appears the weapon bound for the East Coast will be detonated while the ship is in the Canal, closing off the world's major East-West global trade route."

The Premier sat in silence, trying to digest what he had just been told. "And why have the Iraqis come to us with this information instead of going directly to the Americans?" He reached for one of Gao's cigarettes.

"The Iraqis are giving us this information so that *we* can warn the Americans and take credit for preventing the attack. Their thinking is that this would foster a new era of goodwill and allow us to reset our relationship with the U.S. and hasten our global aspirations."

"And what exactly do the Iraqis want in return for this favor, General?"

"The Iraqis want to us to rebuild their infrastructure using our *One Belt One Road* program. They're tired of waiting for the U.S. to do it. Too many broken promises. Iraq needs new bridges, tunnels, power plants, and cargo ports, and they want our money and expertise to get it done. Otherwise, they fear their economy will never get back on its feet."

The two men sat quietly for several minutes, pondering the scenarios. Each puffed patiently on his cigarette. They had been best friends since childhood, and they had risen to power on the coattails of China's most popular leader, President Jiang. Both were outspoken hawks on China's powerful Standing Committee, each with a deep-seeded desire to see China retake its rightful place in the world as a respected twenty-first century superpower.

"Premier Li, there is more to consider here than meets the eye," Gao continued. "The United States is doing everything possible to step on China and prevent our rightful rise to power. If the intelligence on Al-Qaeda is true, an attack of this magnitude on the United States is an opportunity. It would allow us to accelerate our expansion plans by at least a decade."

"You're suggesting that we allow the attack to happen?" the Premier asked thoughtfully.

"Remember what we were able to achieve after the attacks on 9-11? America became so distracted by its wars in the Middle East that our expansion initiatives went unnoticed. Look at what we achieved in Africa, Latin America, and around the South China Sea. Look at all the new markets we developed for our products. We achieved ten years of unfettered expansion before the U.S. finally woke up and realized what was happening," Gao concluded, sitting back in his seat.

"Obama's famous pivot back to Asia was too late," Li mused.

"That's my point."

Another quiet pause ensued as the two men thought some more.

"General," the Premier began, "you are suggesting that we not tell the Americans, correct?"

"Sir, I am suggesting that such an attack is the answer to our problems with the United States. It would give us free reign to achieve all our goals, including the big one."

"Taiwan," Li said.

"Exactly."

"Think about it. An attack of this magnitude against the United States would allow us to take back Taiwan in one fell swoop while the U.S. is distracted elsewhere."

Premier Li put his spent cigarette butt in the ashtray and crossed his legs. "Who knows of this plot, and who has seen the information on the data key?" Li asked.

"Firefly and Panda are the only people besides me who know. I was the only one given a password for the data key. I am certain no one else has seen the details except for Iraqi intelligence."

Li again sat quietly, pondering the outcomes. "General, I'm thinking about the consequences and ramifications of such an attack. I'm sure you have as well. The lives lost. The global market disruption. It would be devastating."

"Indeed, Sir it would. But China has suffered its own devastation over the last one hundred years and nobody seemed to care but us. The British hooked our people on opium and then seized Hong Kong. The Japanese raped and massacred our people at Nanking, and the Americans are determined to use whatever means necessary to prevent our return as a global superpower. The casualties and economic destruction of this Al-Qaeda attack will be significant, and I'm not without feelings for the loss of life and the economic destruction. But an inevitable war between China and the United States could mean the end of civilization itself. Allowing this Al-Qaeda attack to take place may be a way of preventing something much worse."

"I agree with you, my old friend. This is an opportunity, and the Americans have left us no choice. They have held their foot firmly on our necks for decades, and the Blakely Administration has made it clear they intend to hold us down for many years to come with their containment policies, economic tariffs and saber rattling."

Gao silently nodded in agreement.

"I want to make one thing perfectly clear," the Premier said, staring Gao directly in the eye. "The President, must not know anything about this plot or our decision not to tell the Americans. We must make sure we protect him. He is much more than the President to us. We grew up with this man, and we owe our careers to him. Do you understand?"

"Yes, I understand."

"What do you suggest as next steps, General?"

"Sir, we must involve one other Ministry of State Security agent to help manage the flow of information as this attack unfolds and to keep the two of us apprised—on a strictly confidential basis, of course."

"And who do you suggest?" the Premier asked with interest.

"May I suggest the President's son, Jiang Peng? He's our rising star in the Ministry of State Security. He deserves this assignment, and he's like family. We can trust him, and he trusts us."

The Premier nodded silently in agreement. Jiang Peng was only thirty-four years old and on track to take over for General Gao as head of MSS someday. The Premier believed the younger Jiang had the pedigree, influence, and intelligence to follow in his father's footsteps and become President one day. It was a distinct possibility.

"All right, we go with Jiang Peng," the Premier finally said.

The two men stood and shook hands, each with a sense of profound destiny for the People's Republic of China, together with a nervous sense of anticipation over what would happen next. "We'll either be paraded as heroes or duly executed," the Premier murmured to Gao as he led the way out of the meeting room.

★★★

General Gao returned to his office at the Ministry of State Security, relieved that Li had seen things his way. It was an incredibly risky proposition, but the payoff justified the risk. *No one will ever be able to prove that we knew about the plot in advance,* Gao thought as he sat down at his desk. *We will condemn the attacks with the rest of the world and offer our assistance. Then we will move quickly to achieve our global agenda.*

He summoned his secretary. "I need to see Jiang Peng in my office immediately."

SECRETS

CHAPTER 18

Ministry of State Security Headquarters, Beijing, China

Jiang Peng was the oldest son of China's President and a second-generation princeling, the term given to descendants of prominent communist party officials. Tall with an athletic build and clean-cut military features, his quiet demeanor put others at ease. Jiang was surprisingly friendly and modest for a person with such high connections and intelligence. His career was thriving at the Ministry of State Security under the direct tutelage of General Gao Zheng, who was grooming the young man as his successor. It was rare for an MSS Agent to have such broad access to national intelligence. Jiang took it in stride.

Peng possessed a unique understanding of the United States and its culture, having been educated at Milton Academy and later at MIT for graduate studies in computer science. He spoke fluent English and was an expert in American history. It was Peng's vision to someday incorporate the best parts of western liberal democracy into China's one party system to create a kind of political hybrid that the world could respect and embrace.

He had remained friends with his boarding school roommate Jim Keenan, though communications between the two had subsided in recent years as their careers progressed, and security clearances became more of an issue. He often thought back to his days at Milton, recalling the morning of the 9-11 attacks and the time he spent consoling his friend over the news of his father's death.

"Sir, the General would like to see you right away in his office," Peng's secretary said over Jiang's desk intercom.

"Tell him I'm on my way." Jiang took his cell phone and a notepad and headed down the hall.

"Please shut the door and have a seat," Gao said, gesturing to an empty chair across from his desk. "Peng, what I'm about to tell you is highly sensitive. You will be one of only three people who has this top-secret information. And for reasons that will become clear to you, your father is not one of them."

"Yes, sir." He waited expectantly.

"We have intelligence that Al-Qaeda is planning a terrorist attack on the United States. This data storage key contains detailed information about the attack. It was passed on to us from Firefly and Panda in Hong Kong. I need you to review this material and put together a threat assessment on the attack's likelihood and feasibility. Let me reiterate that this is top secret. Your father, the President, must be protected and cannot be made aware of this. It must not leak. Do you understand?"

"Yes, sir. Have we alerted the Americans about the attack yet?"

"We will not be alerting the Americans," Gao replied firmly as he stood to shake hands, signaling the meeting was officially over and that there would be no questions.

Peng asked a question anyway. "Sir, who is the third person who has this information?"

"Premier Li," came the quick reply.

"Please understand our position, Peng. This situation presents us with a major opportunity. It will get the Americans out of our hair for a while so we can achieve our global objectives. I need your best work and your utmost confidence on this."

"Of course, Sir."

Jiang Peng took the data key and walked slowly back to his office at the end of the hall, trying to digest what he had just heard. He inserted the data key into his computer, entered the passcode to open the secret file, and began to read.

ROMEO AND JULIET

CHAPTER 19

Port of Shanghai, China

Ahsan drove alone over the thirty-two-kilometer bridge across Hangzhou Bay out to China's majestic Port of Shanghai. The port handled more than forty million container shipments each year. On this day, Ahsan was interested in only two of them.

He arrived at his office inside the port just in time to see the Iranian ship, *Pasha,* slowly steaming from the outer channel into the terminal operations area. Tugboats gently nudged the containership into docking position under four large cargo cranes alongside Berth 9.

In the clandestine world, Ahsan was known as a *cobbler*. He had a talent for forging passports, drivers' licenses, and shipping documents, all critical to the success of Al-Qaeda's plot to bomb America. A Pakistani accountant by trade, he was a hard-working man in his late thirties who had been radicalized by Jihadists after his parents were killed by a U.S. drone strike in Lahore. The airstrike in the middle of the night hit the wrong house in the wrong neighborhood and killed the wrong people. His people.

Ongoing sanctions against Iran meant that there were only a handful of countries left in the world that would allow Iranian ships to enter. China was one of them. Ahsan had chosen the Port of Shanghai for the mission because of its immense size. It was his *needle in a haystack* strategy—easier to conceal two bad containers among thousands of legitimate ones. Besides, Shanghai offered plenty of choices when it came to choosing ships headed to the United States.

Ahsan's fraudulent documentation was a work of art. On paper, the transaction appeared simple and straightforward. MedTec China was selling two MRI imaging machines to its subsidiary, MedTec USA, in Los Angeles and New York. MedTec was already a legally registered shell company in the United States thanks to Ahsan's handiwork. Several test shipments had been made over the previous six months from Shanghai to the United States, and all had gone smoothly. With an established track record in place for MedTec, the container bombs would easily pass through U.S. Customs and Border Patrol.

Ahsan arranged for the first container bomb unloaded off the *Pasha*, code named *Juliet*, to be transferred over to the German cargo ship *MV Dresden*, which was due to depart Shanghai the next day for New York via the Panama Canal. He arranged for the second container bomb, code named *Romeo*, to be transferred over to the Danish cargo ship *MV Copenhagen*, which would depart for Los Angeles a few days later.

Ahsan was proud of what he had achieved. From his window he watched the *Pasha* being unloaded by cranes in the hazy afternoon sun. The containers were gently lowered onto trucks waiting on the dock below and shuttled over to where the *Dresden* and the *Copenhagen* were docked.

It had taken months of analysis and planning to make Al-Qaeda's nefarious shipments appear legitimate and to synchronize when the bombs would arrive at their intended targets. Ahsan took a deep breath and reflected for a moment on the loss of his parents before sending a coded confirmation text to Al-Qaeda command. "*Romeo and Juliet have crossed the threshold.*"

ANCHORS AWAY

CHAPTER 20

MV *Dresden*: Outbound East China Sea

Captain Franz Hedger stood casually on the bridge of the containership *Dresden.* He looked out over the bow through his Nikon binoculars, scanning for any ship traffic in the vicinity. He was a diminutive man at five foot six, one hundred and sixty pounds, wearing a white, neatly ironed shirt with captain's apelets on the shoulders and dark blue chinos. Born in Warsaw, Poland, Hedger was a graduate of the prestigious Akademia Morska Maritime University in Szczecin, Poland. He had spent more than half of his forty-five years sailing the high seas on containerships. It had been almost ten years since his wife Anika decided to leave him, fed up with the loneliness of a being a mariner's wife. He didn't blame her, and he never remarried. The sea was his mistress, the only place where he ever truly felt happy.

The *MV Dresden* was small in comparison to the latest class of mega ships that had entered service over the last several years. Built in 2007, the ship, owned by Germany's Schiff Lines carried 8,800 cargo containers and could easily fit through the newly expanded locks of the Panama Canal. Weather permitting, the *Dresden* would arrive in Panama in fourteen days, exactly as Ahsan had planned it.

Night fell as the ship got underway. A half-moon lit the sky, casting a glimmering white reflection across the darkness of the open sea. Unknown to Hedger, the *Dresden* was now the equivalent of a nuclear torpedo, with *Juliet* sitting inside container ICLU2236677 and stowed near the bow of the ship.

From the bridge, Hedger could see that they were just about to clear the Port of Shanghai's shipping channel; the final buoy along his starboard side blinked green.

"All ahead fifteen knots," Hedger ordered. It had been a long day, and Hedger found himself in need of a good night's sleep. He turned to his Executive Officer Neil Strahm, who was standing at the helm at the center of the bridge. "I'm going to get some rest, Neil," Hedger said.

"Schlafen sie gut, Captain," came the reply from his XO in German. *Sleep well, Captain.*

As the vessel steamed into calm seas with the moonlight shimmering to the edge of the horizon, Hedger paused to appreciate its beauty. He thought for a brief moment about his wife Anika. *Calm seas never last*, he reminded himself. *Everything is temporary*. For Captain Hedger, the days ahead would once again prove that to be true.

★★★

MV Nordic *Copenhagen*: Outbound ⚓ East China Sea

Two days after the Dresden's departure, Captain Lars Anderson set the *MV Copenhagen* on a northwest course out of Shanghai, destined for the Port of Los Angeles. The voyage would take twelve days, and he knew the route well.

At forty-eight years of age, Anderson was all business. Six foot five with a greying beard, icy blue eyes, and a rugby player build, he was Scandinavian handsome and a commanding presence on the ship's bridge. Anderson was the product of Nordic Lines' rigorous Officer Education Program in Denmark. He had climbed the ranks at Nordic for over twenty-five years and now captained one of the largest and most sophisticated container ships afloat.

At a cost of over $190 million, the *Copenhagen* was one of Nordic's new mega class container ships. It measured over 1300 feet long and 240 feet high with a beam of 193 feet, too wide to fit through the Panama Canal. The *Copenhagen* could carry over 18,000 cargo containers at one time, and despite the ship's enormous size, it was able to safely operate with a crew of just twenty-three people. A small joystick on the ship's bridge replaced the traditional ship wheel, which was noticeably absent.

Onboard Captain Anderson's ship sat *Romeo,* the second of Al-Qaeda's nuclear weapons, destined for downtown Los Angeles. It was nestled in container ICLU265298 and stowed just below the main deck under a massive two-ton hatch cover that separated the ship's upper and lower storage areas.

It was 0200 hours in the morning when the *Copenhagen* finally cleared Shanghai's shipping channel. Like the *Dresden*, the ship was ordered to slow steam at fifteen knots to save on fuel. Anderson, an insomniac and self-described control freak, liked to remain on deck as long as possible while most of his officers preferred going to bed. Getting underway was his favorite part of a voyage, and he didn't want to miss a minute of it. He followed the vessel's progress out to sea on a large GPS moving map at the center of the control console.

"I miss the old maps, don't you?" he asked his Executive Officer, Stephan Jensen.

"Yes, I miss them too, Sir. There is something beautiful about the old way of plotting a ship's course with an actual compass on a physical map," Jensen replied. "Today, we're just robots sailing a giant computer."

The two men stood on the bridge, quietly contemplating the old days of seamanship and enjoying the thrill of again being underway. Unknown to either man was the deadly mission on which the *Copenhagen* had now embarked.

ARREST

CHAPTER 21

John F. Kennedy Airport, New York

On any given day inside JFK's bustling international terminal, thousands of passengers from all corners of the globe arrive for their official customs entry into the United States. On this day, the FBI was interested in just one of those passengers.

Laura Bowman, having arrived from Hong Kong just hours earlier, led a team of six FBI counterterrorism agents into the JFK international arrivals area. They took seats inside the Customs and Border Patrol office within the airport's immigration section. Chatting quietly, they awaited news on the arrival of Cathay Pacific flight 888 from Hong Kong, which was running fifteen minutes late.

Agent Kate Spellman, who was monitoring the flight's status from the control tower, radioed Bowman.

"Confirm CX flight is on the ground and taxiing to Gate 43," Spellman announced.

"We're on," Bowman informed her team.

The agents rose from their seats, exited through the office doors, and quickly got into position. They needed to act fast in apprehending Kwok as soon as he cleared immigration. He had flown business class per Rothchild's executive travel policy, which meant he would be one of the first passengers off the plane when it arrived at Gate 43 and one of the first passengers to enter the immigration hall.

Watching expectantly, Bowman spotted Kwok walking purposefully toward the inspection area while fumbling for his passport. He was wearing a grey t-shirt with loose chinos and an old Yankees baseball hat.

"This is it," Bowman announced to the team on her headset. "Remember—we take him quickly and quietly. No commotion."

Kwok spoke briefly with the border patrol officer who was reviewing his passport.

"What do you do for employment, Mr. Kwok?" the officer asked.

"I run cybersecurity for Rothchild's in Hong Kong."

The Customs officer glanced at the photo on Kwok's passport and held it up to see that it matched with his actual face. "Welcome back," the agent said, handing Kwok his passport and giving no hint as to what would happen next.

"Nice to be back," Kwok replied respectfully. He walked past the Customs booth and turned left down a narrow corridor toward the baggage claim area.

As Kwok turned the corner, Bowman and the FBI team consolidated their positions around him, holding their badges in the air, as Laura ordered him to freeze.

"Mr. Kwok, I'm Special Agent in Charge Laura Bowman from the Federal Bureau of Investigation. You are under arrest for espionage against the United States of America."

Kwok showed no emotion. He put his hands behind his back and was placed in handcuffs while Bowman read him his Rights. The agents, dressed in blue jackets with yellow FBI initials on the back, briskly walked the prisoner to a nearby exit door where three black suburban SUVs were waiting.

"Watch your head, please, Mr. Kwok," Bowman advised as they tucked him into the middle seat of the lead suburban and shut the door. The caravan sped off for the General Aviation terminal on the other side of JFK Airport to meet a private FBI Gulfstream jet sitting ready on the tarmac.

Kwok was escorted up the steps of the G5's open hatch. His handcuffs were reversed from back to front to allow his arms to rest on his lap during the flight. He was buckled into the first seat on the airplane's right side next to a large oval window.

Two security agents buckled in next to him.

"Would you like some water, Mr. Kwok?" Bowman asked.

There was no reply.

Bowman took a seat toward the back of the plane and phoned Keenan. "Jim, we have him. We're on our way," she stated with a deep feeling of accomplishment.

"Great. I'm at the Shangri-La Hotel," he shot back jokingly.

"You wish," she said, smiling.

They received immediate takeoff clearance from ATC and departed for the forty-five-minute hop to Washington. Bowman sat back in her seat, the adrenaline rushing through her body keeping her wide awake. *I have a new cure for jet lag to tell Jim about*, she thought, looking out the window above the early morning clouds.

★★★

DCA Reagan National Airport, Washington D.C.

The Gulfstream touched down smoothly at Washington's Reagan National Airport and rolled down the runway before turning left and entering an FBI secure hanger. Inside the hanger, three more Chevy suburbans were waiting.

Bowman opened the hatch and walked down the steps first.

The two security agents appeared at the jet's door minutes later, holding Kwok's handcuffed arms on either side and helping him down the steps. He was seated inside the second vehicle and strapped in.

Bowman got in on Kwok's left side, putting on her Ray Ban aviator sunglasses, wishing Jim could see how good she looked wearing them.

"Ready to go," she confirmed to the team on her radio. "How are you feeling, Mr. Kwok?" Bowman politely inquired. Again, there was no response.

With police blue and red lights flashing, the small caravan of SUV's left the jet hanger for the thirty-minute drive to the FBI's Training Academy in Quantico, Virginia. A long list of questions awaited Henry Kwok, and a long line of people who were eager for answers.

THE ROOM BEHIND THE MIRROR

CHAPTER 22

FBI Training Academy, Quantico Virginia

In a small, windowless interrogation room thirty-six miles south of Washington D.C., Henry Kwok sat alone and struggled to concentrate. As a trained CIA officer, he was familiar with the interrogation process and remained calm, but the initial rush of being arrested had long since worn off, and his eight-thousand-mile trip was taking its toll . His metal chair was uncomfortable, and he fidgeted to find a better position. He faced a two-way mirror on the far wall. A video camera and microphone had been set up to record the interview.

Laura Bowman sat in the viewing room behind the two-way mirror along with her boss, FBI counterintelligence Chief Richard Holmes. She was still in the clothes she had worn from Hong Kong, but she felt refreshed and alert. Tom Fahey and Jim Keenan joined, which made the room feel cramped.

The High Value Detainee Interrogation Group, otherwise known as the *HIG*, had been in existence since 2009. It was created to maximize the effectiveness of interrogation techniques by combining the skill sets of the FBI, CIA, and the Department of Defense. The man responsible for leading the HIG was FBI chief interrogator Brian Connelly, who in the school of interrogations was in a class by himself. He had spent a career perfecting his craft in Guantanamo Bay, Iraq, and Afghanistan. He was the best in the business.

A slight, unassuming man in his mid-sixties, gray and balding with black-rim glasses and trusting brown eyes, he looked more like a small-town dentist who pulled teeth than a man who specialized in extracting information. In addition to the FBI, Connelly taught interrogation techniques at the CIA's training center called The Farm at Camp Peary in Williamsburg, Virginia. He was only brought into active investigations in special circumstances, and the interrogation of Henry Kwok more than qualified as a special circumstance. Connelly joined the others in the overcrowded viewing room for a pre-interrogation briefing.

"Okay folks, we need to understand that interrogations are a team effort," Connelly began as if teaching one of his classes. "Your role today is to actively listen to how Kwok answers my questions and identify any gaps," he continued. "I'm going to try and build a rapport with Kwok by laying out the facts as we know them, and then get his narrative on what's happened in China. Does that make sense?"

Everyone nodded in agreement like third graders.

"It's critical that I make a good first impression and set the tone. We're fortunate to have a comprehensive dossier on Mr. Kwok, which I've gone over in detail with the other members of the HIG Group from Langley and the Pentagon. He is an experienced intelligence agent, and it will be important he not feel coerced. He needs to feel that he has a certain level of autonomy and control over the situation. Are you with me?"

Again, the students murmured assent.

"I'm going to use what we call a funnel method of questioning, starting with open-ended questions, gradually narrowing the scope down to what we are trying to get at. I will introduce the evidence to him, which includes the gambling debts, phone calls, and of course, the notebook. I will also make it clear that the latest amendment to the Patriot Act calls for a mandatory death sentence for the crime of treason to give him some food for thought. Questions?"

"A quick question, Brian," Tom Fahey interjected. "As you mentioned, Kwok is an experienced intelligence officer. How effective can you be with someone who knows the drill?"

"Sometimes we get lucky and this process allows bad agents to relieve themselves of all the stress and guilt they have been carrying around. There is only one way to find out. Shall we get started?"

Connelly entered the interrogation room carrying a Dunkin Donuts coffee and wearing a relaxed white button-down collar shirt, blue blazer, and khaki chinos.

Keenan focused on Connelly's choice of white socks and black shoes, which reminded him of Charlie O'Flaherty's China Vuitton description. *Same thrift shop,* he smirked.

Dunkin Donuts was Kwok's favorite coffee with a cream and two sugars, which Connelly already knew from the dossier. "Here you go, Henry" Connelly said, gently placing the coffee on the table in front of Kwok. "My name is Brian Connelly, and I'm with the FBI's interrogation unit." He unlocked Kwok's handcuffs and started the video camera and recorder.

"Before we begin, I want to confirm that you've been read your rights and that you understand them. Is that correct, Henry?"

"Yes," Kwok replied, sipping his coffee. He had heard stories about the infamous Brian Connelly but had never seen him in action. *At least they sent their best to deal with me,* he thought.

"I also want to make you aware that under the revised Patriot Act, the crime of treason now carries a mandatory death sentence. Do you understand that?"

"Yes," Kwok murmured, unaware that was the case.

Kwok then spoke up. "And do you understand, Mr. Connelly, that I demand to see a lawyer right now?"

Connelly smiled and briefly left the room. He returned with the federal defense attorney that had been pre-arranged in anticipation of such a request from the detainee.

"Mr. Kwok, I'm attorney Ian Daniels, I was court appointed and I will be representing you, at least for the time being."

Daniels sat down in the only empty chair left in the room.

"Now, where were we?" Connelly muttered sarcastically, "Ah yes, the death penalty. We do executions *old school* for treason, Henry. Death by electrocution at Sing Sing Prison in New York. Two cycles of 1750 volts each while sitting on old sparky. Same chair that was used for Julius and Ethyl Rosenberg. Did you know Ethel had to be put back in the chair and zapped again after they found her heart was still beating? Nasty stuff. Time is of the essence here. We need you to cooperate. So why don't you tell me everything you know about what's happened in China related to PROJECT LUCY?"

"And what if I tell you to fuck off instead?" Kwok shot back.

"So much for rapport building," Keenan blurted out from behind the two-way mirror.

Kwok tried to remain calm, but he was feeling nauseous, and the thought of 1750 volts of electricity running through his body wasn't helping matters.

"You worked directly for Jim Keenan at the CIA China Desk, correct?" Connelly continued.

"Yes."

"You worked specifically on PROJECT LUCY, and you knew the identities of our assets working this operation in China, including the twelve people that have been killed."

"No," Henry Kwok answered. "That information was top secret and beyond my clearance."

"After you were fired from the Agency for drinking and gambling violations, you accepted two wire payments totaling about $20,000 from an HSBC account in Hong Kong. That $20,000 coincidentally covered your gambling debts at the Mohegan Sun Casino in Connecticut."

"Yes."

"A few weeks later, you accepted a job with Rothchild's Auction House in Hong Kong, and you relocated your family there?"

"Yes," Kwok repeated.

"But before you got to Hong Kong, you stopped in Bali for a family vacation, and that's where we found this." He pulled out a photo of the notebook found in his hotel and placed it in front of Kwok and his attorney.

Kwok suddenly pictured himself strapped in the electric chair with a wet sponge placed on his head and a dark hood being pulled over his face.

Connelly continued, "It so happens that the names and numbers of the people listed in your little notebook here are the same people who have been shot."

The notebook was a surprise, and Kwok's skin turned cold and clammy. His heart raced, and his dry mouth made his tongue stick to his upper palate.

"This little notebook, Henry, is why we're giving you one last chance, right now, to tell us everything you know so that we can save the lives of our remaining assets in China. And I don't need to remind you, but I will, about what the Chinese PLA will do to your family in Hong Kong when they find out we have you in custody and that you're talking to us."

"This guy is good," Bowman said to the others standing behind the mirror in amazement.

Kwok's hands and legs began to tremble uncontrollably, and he did a poor job hiding it.

"So here is the deal, Henry. You tell us everything we want to know right now, and we will get your family out of Hong Kong and bring them to the United States. They will be safe here, and you can see them again. That's it. That's the deal. I'll give you a few minutes to speak alone with your attorney, and then it's show time, as they say." Connelly stood up. "You've got thirty minutes," he said, opening the door. "And as my mother used to say, make good choices."

★★★

Lawyer-client privilege meant that the team behind the mirror could no longer listen in on the conversation in the interrogation room, and the recorder was turned off.

Attorney Ian Daniels spoke to Kwok in a soft and comforting tone. "Henry, it's true that under the new law the crime of treason is a mandatory death sentence. It was added to the Patriot Act by President Blakely last year. It's never been tested in the courts, so there is a chance you could avoid execution, but they already have you recorded in a lie, and they're pretty upset over losing twelve of their people. I suggest you take their offer and tell them all you know. You may not be able to save yourself, but you can at least save your family. The death penalty appeals process will drag on for decades in your favor. You're realistically looking at a life sentence."

It suddenly occurred to Kwok that something was not quite right. The interrogation had been entirely focused on the dead CIA assets and PROJECT LUCY. There was no mention of an imminent Al-Qaeda terrorist threat against the United States. He hadn't been asked a single question about Beijing's knowledge of a terrorist plot. Then it suddenly hit him. *They haven't asked me about China and the Al-Qaeda plot because Beijing never informed Washington! These guys have no fucking idea they're about to be attacked.* He suddenly felt a sense of relief realizing he had enough leverage to avoid the electric chair.

Kwok turned to Attorney Daniels with a mischievous grin.

"The CIA is concerned about the loss of their twelve assets in China, right?

"That's right. Plus, their eight remaining assets"

"Well, I have information that could save millions of American lives right here at home," Kwok said, eager to get Connelly back in the room.

"What did you say?"

"I have information about an imminent terrorist attack by Al-Qaeda against the United States that's going to make September 11th look like a minor traffic accident. I know for a fact that Beijing is withholding critical information from the United States. You go tell the people behind the mirror over there that I'm willing to tell them what I know, but no death penalty. In fact, I want complete immunity, and I want my family evacuated out of Hong Kong right away."

"Let me have a word with them," Daniels said abruptly as he rose to leave the room.

"Mr. Daniels, with what I know about the timing of this Al-Qaeda attack, you'd better fucking hurry."

★★★

After a quick briefing by Daniels to the team in the viewing room, Bowman, Keenan, Fahey, and Holmes all joined Daniels in the crowded interrogation room.

Tom Fahey took over the conversation. "Henry, you are requesting immunity, which is simply not possible given that you've committed treason against the United States of America."

"Well, then, what's about to happen is on you, Tommy," Kwok replied sharply.

"If you can be more specific about the information you have regarding an attack, we might be able to consider life in prison."

"When you hear what I have to say, you will grant me immunity," Kwok replied.

"Can you give us a hint, Henry?"

Kwok took a sip of coffee. He sat back in his chair and looked at each of the agents one by one before he began.

"Al-Qaeda has a plot underway to attack two locations in the United States. They plan to cripple America and the entire global economy."

"And how do you know this?"

"I was the go-between that relayed details of the attack from Iraq's Intelligence Service to Beijing."

"Wait a minute, Henry. You're saying there is a terrorist plot against the United States—and Beijing is aware of it?"

"Yes, that's what I'm telling you. And that's not all," Kwok continued. "The attack will use nuclear weapons."

The room went silent. Attorney Daniels spoke first. "I believe my client has told you enough for you to grant immunity. Whatever you decide, you'd better make it quick."

"Okay, shithead," Fahey shot back. "If what you are telling us is true, and we get full disclosure on every detail you have right fucking now, then we are prepared to grant immunity. If this is a bunch of bullshit, then I will personally come to your cell and kill you myself."

★★★

"Let's start at the beginning," Connelly said, trying to return to an atmosphere of rapport building. "Tell us what you know."

"I was instructed by my Beijing handler to meet with a female Iraqi agent for lunch in Hong Kong last week," Kwok began.

"Who is your handler?" Bowman interjected.

"I only know him by his code name, Panda."

Bowman made a mental connection and opened a folder of photographs she had taken in Hong Kong. She pulled out one of the photos of Kwok sitting at the noodle shop. "Is this the female Iraqi agent you're talking about?" Bowman asked.

"That's her."

Bowman showed the photo around to the others in the room.

"During our meeting she handed me a computer storage key with specific data about the Al-Qaeda plot, and she gave me highlights of the attack during our conversation." Bowman again reached in her folder, pulling out a photograph that clearly showed the data key being handed over to Kwok at the restaurant. She passed the photo around. His story was holding up so far.

"And why would the Iraqis give this information to Beijing instead of to Washington?" Brian Connelly asked.

"As best as I can determine, the Iraqis are looking for a quid pro quo. They're giving Beijing the opportunity to play the hero by informing the U.S. of the impending attack, thereby gaining huge street cred and goodwill. Beijing would theoretically achieve a new kind of negotiating leverage with America on just about everything."

"And what the fuck does Iraq get out of this ridiculous tactic?" Fahey asked.

"Iraq is asking China to rebuild their country's entire infrastructure from top to bottom as part of the One Belt / One Road initiative. They believe if China is willing to build new ports and roads in places like Pakistan and

Africa, then they should be willing to rebuild Iraq. They are expecting China to fund all the construction as well."

"And what about details on the attack?" Keenan asked.

"The Iraqi agent made it clear that Al-Qaeda somehow got their hands on two tactical nuclear weapons which they plan to use. The nukes will most likely be dropped from airplanes or loaded onto commercial airliners and flown into targets like on 9-11," Kwok continued, adding his own unsubstantiated assessment.

"This can't be happening again," Keenan whispered to himself.

Fahey continued, "You handed over all this information to your Beijing handler days ago. Why haven't we heard anything from the fucking Chinese?" he asked, looking around the room at all the pissed-off faces.

"I was wondering the same thing," Kwok replied.

★★★

Tom Fahey's phone began to vibrate, the name "Charles Wentworth" appearing across the screen as he answered.

"Sir, we're here with Kwok right now," Fahey said leaving the interrogation room to go out into the hallway. Keenan followed Fahey into the hallway and closed the door behind him. "I have Jim with me, Sir. What's up?"

"Gentlemen, we just received word from the Israelis that a Mossad commando team raided a facility located under an archeological dig called Persepolis in Iran yesterday. The Israelis had evidence indicating nuclear weapons were secretly being stored there. When the commandos arrived at the site, they found the facility had recently been broken into and robbed. At least that's what it looked like. Whatever was being stored there was gone."

"Wow," was all Fahey could muster recalling his recent conversation with Mossad.

"There's more, Tom. All the background chatter and government conversations we've been monitoring in Tehran since yesterday indicate the nuclear weapons did in fact exist, and that they are missing. As of thirty minutes ago, Iranian television has begun publicly claiming that Israel stole their nuclear weapons. CNN has just gone to breaking news with the story. Guys, there are at least two rogue weapons out there. We have no idea where they are or who has them."

Keenan's mind raced in silence, piecing together Wentworth's news with Henry Kwok's disturbing revelation. Fahey was doing the same thing.

"Sir, Jim Keenan here. We need to brief you and the President right away. It appears from what Kwok is telling us, together with this latest intelligence from Mossad, that the United States is in grave danger of a nuclear terrorist attack, and we may not have much time."

"Meet me at the White House in one hour," Wentworth said, ending the call.

PREPARATIONS

CHAPTER 23

The White House

CIA Director Wentworth had the unenviable task of advising the President on the shocking revelations out of Israel and the confession of Henry Kwok. He gave the rest of the government a head-start on the alarming news so that national security precautions could be activated without delay.

Wentworth arrived at the White House at 1615 hours along with Fahey, Keenan, and Laura Bowman. They briefed the President privately in the Oval Office before moving to the Situation Room where FBI Director Kendall, Department of Homeland Security Director Ben Halsey, Secretary of Defense Lindsey Metcalf, and the President's Chief of Staff Chris Dodd were already waiting.

A cacophony of chatter resonated throughout the crowded room until the President arrived. He took his seat and watched as everyone else took theirs. Administrative staff without a seat stood along the perimeter.

The flat screen TVs mounted on the four walls around the situation room were tuned to CNN and FOX News. The volumes were all muted, but the reporting from the White House lawn and the news streaming across the bottom of the screens made it clear that something big was happening—and nobody was sure what it was. On Wall Street, the S&P 500 had plunged 30% before the closing bell.

"Okay, what are we looking at?" POTUS asked no one in particular.

DHS Director Halsey was the first to speak. "Mr. President, we've initiated the BADGER PROTOCOL, putting us at the highest threat level across the country. Together with the FAA we've grounded all domestic flights, and all inbound international flights have been diverted out of U.S. airspace. We understand the Israelis have done the same."

"And at this point the public has no idea why we're taking these precautions?" POTUS asked for clarification.

"That's right, Sir," Chris Dodd chimed in. "We thought it best for you to address the Nation as soon as possible. The question is how much detail we want to divulge to the public given the level of panic that will ensue," his Chief of Staff continued.

"Sir, we can try to conceal the nuclear nature of the threat, but it's only a matter of time before the media makes the connection between the stolen nukes in Iran and our highest threat preparedness level," Secretary of Defense Metcalf added.

"Mr. President, we've scheduled you to address the Nation live at 7PM Eastern," Chris Dodd said. "We're working on the messaging now with our communications team."

"I think we need to know a lot more detail about the credibility of this threat before we start telling Americans they could be nuked," POTUS said in an unusually thoughtful tone. "We should warn the public to be vigilant about a potential terrorist attack without giving any alarming specifics that haven't been verified. We don't want the panic to be worse than the perceived threat."

"Yes, Sir. That's what DHS would recommend as well," Secretary Halsey added.

"We've already locked down the National airspace," Halsey continued. "If Al-Qaeda has sent tactical nukes into the United States, they are either sitting in airplanes we've already grounded, or they're in the planes we diverted to other countries. Sir, we need an executive order to search the cargo holds of every aircraft that's come into the United States from overseas since last week. We should recommend other countries do the same. And we need to seize the cargo manifests of all inbound aircraft to trace where their cargo went after being unloaded. If there are nuclear weapons out there, they will give off a traceable radioactive signature that our scanning equipment should be able to detect," Halsey concluded, leaning back.

"Sort of pissing into the wind, isn't it, Ben?" Metcalf asked. "Even a shipment of bananas gives off a radioactive signature, doesn't it?"

"That's true, Lindsey. And if you have a better idea on what to do next, I'm all ears."

"And what do we do when we find the nukes, Mr. Halsey?" POTUS asked.

"We'll take it from there, Sir," Secretary of Defense Metcalf added firmly. "We have special personnel that can defuse these types of weapons. You know. Hurt Locker types."

"Any objections?" POTUS asked, looking around the room.

There were none.

"Okay, I want DOD and DHS to work hand in hand to do the search. I want updates every hour," POTUS ordered. "And Chris, I need a draft of tonight's speech soonest, so we can review it and get the messaging right."

"I'm on it, Sir," his Chief of Staff quickly replied.

The President shifted in his chair, leaned his elbows on the conference room table, and looked over at Wentworth and Kendall.

"Now, can someone please tell me why the fucking Chinese and Iraqis chose not to warn us about this attack?" Blakely bellowed in a strong Alabama accent, his face red and eyes bulging with anger.

"We're not sure," Charles Wentworth volunteered. "All we know is that Henry Kwok's story of an imminent nuclear attack by Al-Qaeda lines up with the intelligence we've just received from Israel."

"I want a phone call set up with that commie shit President ASAP. But I need to be sure this Kwok story is true. If it turns out to be a bunch of bullshit, I'm going to look like a foolish ass in front of the Chinese. Do I look like a foolish ass to you, Chuck?"

"No, Sir," Wentworth replied as everyone in the room began to uncomfortably fidget in their seats.

"Well, I'm glad to hear that, Chuck," POTUS concluded.

"Sir, as you know, Agent Bowman and I were the ones who surveilled Kwok in Hong Kong," Keenan interjected. "We can confirm he met with an Iraqi agent, and we can confirm he received a data storage key that was passed on to Beijing. There is no doubt. The Chinese have the detailed information we need about the attack."

"Then why the fuck haven't they told us about it, Jim?" POTUS asked in an irritated tone.

"They must have determined that an attack on the United States would somehow be in their best interest," Tom Fahey advised.

"So, what do we do about it?" POTUS asked.

"We need to let the Chinese know that we're on to them. Get them to admit they have the information and convince them they need to give it to us as soon as possible. Sir, we need you to call President Jiang and put the pressure on now," Keenan concluded.

"Then set up the damn call," POTUS demanded. "The Secretary of State is enroute to Israel, but we can't afford to wait for him."

"There is one more thing, Mr. President," Wentworth added. "Henry Kwok is giving us extremely valuable information, but we had to make a deal with him for his cooperation. Part of that deal is we have to extract his family out of Hong Kong right away before the Chinese take them hostage. The other part of the deal is we're going to have to grant him immunity, I'm afraid."

"Thanks for letting me know, Chuck," POTUS said with a level of agitation.

There was a brief pause in the discussion as the President tried to digest all that was happening.

"Secretary Metcalf," POTUS said in a somber tone. "I need a briefing in the next two hours from someone at DOD who knows exactly what we can expect if nuclear weapons start detonating in U.S. cities. I need blast scenarios, casualty statistics, immediate and long-term impact. And Lindsey, don't sugarcoat it."

"Right away, Mr. President," Metcalf answered as the meeting temporarily adjourned.

★★★

MV Copenhagen: Pacific Ocean

The *MV Copenhagen* was slow steaming at fifteen knots in six-foot seas. The weather had been favorable across the Pacific, and the ship was right on schedule. Exactly what Captain Anderson had built his reputation on.

"Sir, our coordinates are set for the approach channel into the Port of Los Angeles," the ship's XO Stephen Jensen called out from across the bridge. "We anticipate no delays at this time, Sir."

"Very well," came the quick reply.

★★★

MV Dresden: Southern Pacific Ocean

Captain Hedger stood on the bridge of the *MV Dresden* looking out on the high seas and contemplating another successful voyage. He would be flying back to Germany when the ship reached New York, and he was looking forward to getting some time off. The *Dresden* was slightly behind schedule, but with a small increase in speed the ship would make it to the approach channel of the Panama Canal as planned.

"Increase speed to twenty knots and inform the Canal Authority of our position and estimated time of arrival, please," Hedger instructed his Executive Officer on the bridge.

"Stetig wie sie geht," Hedger added in German.

Steady as she goes.

MY FELLOW AMERICANS

CHAPTER 24

At 1800 hours the leadership team reassembled in the Situation Room to hear from Lindsey Metcalf and the expert on nuclear weapons she brought in from the Pentagon. It was an hour before POTUS was scheduled to address the nation.

"Sir, I'm Colonel David Dunn from Strategic Air Command. I specialize in nuclear threat assessments."

Dunn was a nerdy-looking man who still used a pocket protector. He had a reputation around the Pentagon for being a kind of dark cloud, which wasn't unusual given what he did for a living. He had given so many doom and gloom assessments on nuclear annihilation that the Army referred to him as "All Dunn."

"Colonel, I want you to tell us what we could be facing here in the event of a nuke attack, and don't water it down," POTUS directed, sitting back in his chair.

"Sir, we've done quite a bit of work over the years in modeling a terrorist nuclear attack. For our modeling purposes, we assume the bad guys use a crudely made ten-kiloton tactical nuke."

"Crudely made?"

"Yes, Sir. It's easier to make an unpredictable nuclear weapon than it is to make a reliable one, but the destruction caused by a crudely made nuke can be just as devastating as any other nuke, if it works."

"And what does it involve?" POTUS asked, leaning forward to listen carefully.

"Well, Sir, it involves taking a piece of highly enriched uranium 235 that is roughly the size of a bowling ball and detonating it, using conventional explosives. Our modeling assumes that the terrorists place this type of dirty bomb in a van or truck and drive it into a crowded city before triggering the device. We have not modeled any scenarios where a tactical nuclear weapon is dropped from an airplane. We do know that an airburst just a couple of thousand feet above a city would be much more destructive than a ground blast."

"And assuming a ten-kiloton weapon is detonated in, say, Manhattan, what can we expect?"

"To put it in perspective, a ten-kiloton weapon is equivalent to 10,000 tons of conventional explosives. In a nano-second upon detonation, temperature and pressure inside the uranium would reach levels equivalent to the center of the sun just before an immense energy release and explosion occurs in an outward direction. There would be a massive blast, followed by a wave of intense heat and highly lethal radiation. A large fireball would erupt, killing everyone within it, and this would produce the signature mushroom cloud we all associate with a nuclear blast. The blast wave after the initial detonation would create what we call an overpressure, which would obliterate buildings up to a mile out from ground zero."

"Go on." The President's eyes were riveted on Dunn as he spoke.

"Ionized plasma inside the fireball would generate an electromagnetic pulse that would knock out all electronics and communication equipment within a fifty-mile radius of the blast. There would be an enormous burst of gamma and neutron radiation that would instantly kill everyone within a half mile of ground zero. The brilliant flash at detonation would blind anyone who looked at it. Those caught inside the blast zone would be vaporized."

The attendees around the Situation Room table listened in silent horror as Colonel Dunn continued his gruesome analysis.

"Anything else, Colonel?" POTUS asked, knowing there would be more.

"Well, Sir, we can expect that a secondary firestorm would erupt as gas lines and other flammable types of infrastructure, such as oil refineries, start to explode. As the heat from all the fire sources begins to rise, hurricane-force winds would develop and intensify the effects."

"I think we get the picture, Colonel," POTUS interjected.

"Sir, there is one more thing you should know."

"And what is that, Colonel?" POTUS asked, taking a sip of water.

"Mr. President, the scenario I've just outlined is based on our modeling of a ten-kiloton nuclear device. We believe an Iranian-developed nuclear weapon would be more comparable to what Pakistan has been able to develop."

"And what does that mean?" Blakely asked intently.

"We believe the yields on any Iranian-developed nukes would be much bigger than ten kilotons."

"How big, Colonel?"

Dunn paused. "We should expect their weapons to be in the 25- to 150-kiloton range. Expected casualties in a city like Manhattan would be one million citizens in the first week. Long-term radiation deaths would be much more."

"So, the scenario you just outlined for us with a ten-kiloton bomb would be the equivalent of a firecracker compared to what we may actually be looking at here."

"That's one way of putting it, Sir."

"Thank you," POTUS said as he rose to his feet while everyone in the room reflexively stood with him.

"I have to go on television now and try to convince the American people to remain calm. I hope to God they don't see the fear on my face."

As POTUS walked to the door he stopped and turned back to Dunn. "Colonel, out of curiosity, where did the Pakistanis and Iranians get the enriched uranium and technical expertise needed to build their nuclear weapons?"

"From China, Sir."

★★★

In the Oval Office, President Blakley sat uncomfortably upright behind the Resolute Desk and timidly faced the television camera. On the periphery of the Oval stood Wentworth, Fahey, Keenan, and Bowman along with Metcalf, Kendall, and Dodd. POTUS waited impatiently for Kim Blazer, the White House Communications Director, to give the thumbs up to begin his speech.

"In three, two, one…you're on, Sir."

President Blakely began to speak calmly but forcefully. "My fellow Americans, today on my orders, the Department of Homeland Security and the United States Armed Forces initiated the highest level of precautionary measures to ensure the safety and security of our citizens against the threat of a terrorist incident. We have intelligence that suggests Al-Qaeda is planning an attack on the United States. The location and nature of the attack is unknown at this time. We have chosen to take the side of caution by temporarily shutting down our domestic and international airspace until we can be sure it is safe and secure."

He paused to let this sink in.

"As Americans in the post 9-11 world, we have been through security threat levels in the past. The steps we have taken today are temporary and precautionary. It is important that we continue to go about our daily lives. At the same time, we ask that you remain vigilant and report anything suspicious to your local authorities. The war on terror has no frontline. Our enemies continue to try and disrupt our American way of life and our freedoms. The only way they win is if we let them win."

The cameras angled closer to his face.

"Rest assured that my Administration, together with our military and intelligence agencies, are doing everything possible at home and abroad to protect our citizens against the threat of terrorism. This is a battle we must win, and with your help, this is a battle we will win. God bless you, and God bless the United States of America."

As the television lights switched off, Keenan was staring at Laura Bowman in utter disbelief that the President's message had been so unalarming, uninformative, and misleading. *Precautionary measures?* Keenan thought. He pulled Communications Director Blazer aside. "Susan, we're looking at the possibility of a million people being vaporized or poisoned by radiation, and POTUS just gave the country the equivalent of a strong wind advisory," Keenan whispered.

"I hear you, Jim. The Administration doesn't want to panic the country," she whispered back. "I tried. Believe me I tried."

EXTRACTION

CHAPTER 25

Hong Kong SAR:

Elaine Kwok followed the urgent instructions sent by her husband via WhatsApp. She took her two children and stood across the street from Smugglers Bar in the small Hong Kong village of Stanley at exactly 4:00 PM.

The street, a popular destination for tourists and locals, was crowded with cars and foot traffic. A blue unmarked van pulled over directly in front of where the Kwok family stood. As the van's doors slid open, a tall western man in a baseball cap and dark sunglasses got out and walked directly toward the family.

"Ms. Kwok, I'm Agent Rowinski with the U.S. Consulate. You and your family are in danger, and I don't have time to explain it right now. By order of the State Department, I'm to get you and your family to the airport immediately, so we can get you back with your husband

Henry in the United States." Rowinski gently began guiding Kwok and her children toward the vehicle.

"Where is my husband?" she asked, resisting pressure to get into the van.

"Ma'am, your husband is safe. He is with our team in Washington DC, and he wants you to follow our instructions. For your safety and the safety of your family, please get in the van."

She took her small boys by the hand and got in. Rowinski quickly closed the door, and they began the fifty-minute drive to Chek Lap Kok Airport.

As they approached the airport, Mrs. Kwok noticed they weren't heading toward the main terminal. "Where are we going?" she asked. "Why aren't we going to the airline drop-off area?" The van sped down a side street parallel to the main runway before pulling into the general aviation terminal where Hong Kong's billionaire tycoons kept their private jets.

A U.S. Navy C-2 Greyhound sat waiting for them, its twin propellers churning noisily. Built in the 1960s, the C2 was still being used by the Navy to transport crews and cargo to and from aircraft carriers. Pilots affectionately referred to the plane as the *whistling shitcan*.

The Kwok family was escorted onto the aircraft through a rear cargo door that was lowered to the tarmac, revealing the plane's primitive jump seats that faced the rear. The windowless interior resembled an unfinished high school science project. Exposed electrical wiring and hydraulic tubing hung from the ceiling. A crude ladder was used to access the cockpit.

The Kwok's were fitted with green LPU-32 floatation devices left over from the Vietnam war, earplugs, and white safety deck helmets before being strapped into their seats by Navy crew members.

"Where are we going?" Mrs. Kwok repeated over the noise of the propellers.

"Ma'am, we're taking you to the USS Nimitz," Agent Rowinski finally said. "It's an aircraft carrier 250 miles off the coast in the South China Sea. The flight will take about an hour. From there you will fly to Japan and then take a commercial flight to Washington D.C."

The cargo door closed, and the plane immediately taxied to Runway 07R for a pre-cleared military departure. The plane slowly lifted off the runway into the hazy afternoon sky.

Back in Washington, Keenan's phone chimed with a text message from Rowinski.

"Mama Bear and Cubs are safely out of the woods."

Keenan read it and felt relieved. He quickly got word of the successful extraction to Henry Kwok who was sitting in his cell at Quantico.

The Oval Office

Arranging a call with China's President Jiang didn't take long. POTUS and the Chinese President had met on several occasions over the previous three years, and they had developed a cordial relationship despite Blakely's disdain for everything Beijing.

The Chinese had never dealt with a U.S. President quite like Robert J. Blakely. The psychological profile on him conducted by China's Ministry of State Security concluded that Blakely suffered from, among other things, megalomania and narcissism. The MSS's final conclusion, when translated into English, was that Blakely had a screw loose.

It had taken awhile to brief POTUS on how the conversation should go, mainly because of his anger and agitation. "If this shit is true about China protecting Al-Qaeda, I'm going to personally fly over there and stick a hot cattle prod up that little commie's ass," POTUS yelled from the bathroom just outside the Oval Office as the call was being placed.

"Sir, we have President Jiang on the line," came the announcement from the State Department's Liaison Officer, Sheldon Katz. The President had decided to take the call in the confines of the Oval Office instead of being surrounded by an audience in the Situation Room. National Security Advisor Steven Berger joined Charles Wentworth, Fahey, and FBI Director Kendall. As was customary on such calls with heads of state, several other government officials from the intelligence and defense communities would be listening in and taking notes.

"Neeeee Howww," POTUS opened with a pitiful attempt at saying "hello" in Mandarin. "President Blakely, to what do we owe the honor of this call?" the Chinese leader politely replied in near-perfect English.

"We've got a little problem over here, Mr. President," POTUS continued.

"Yes, we've been watching the news," Jiang replied, "and we're all deeply concerned about this threat against the United States. How can we help?"

POTUS turned to his prepared speaking notes that had been written for him by the State Department. "President Jiang, our intelligence here indicates that your government may have information that could help us prevent this attack," POTUS said.

The phone line went silent for a moment as China's President tried to process what he had just heard. "President Blakely, I can assure you that if we had such information, you would have received it already."

"Well," POTUS continued, "we have a reliable source and photographs of a meeting that took place in Hong Kong between an Iraqi intelligence agent and a person from your Ministry of State Security, who by the way, used to work for us. I believe your code name for him is Firefly."

Jiang was silent.

POTUS went on. "We have photos of a computer data storage key being given to Firefly by the Iraqi agent, and we know it contains critical information about Al-Qaeda 's plot. The Iraqi agent also informed Firefly verbally about certain aspects of the plot."

Jiang's face tightened, but he struggled to remain cordial. "President Blakely, are you suggesting that the People's Republic of China wants to see America attacked?

I find this accusation highly insulting and without any basis in fact."

"Well let me fill you in on a little secret Jiang, your double agent Firefly is at this very moment sitting with our FBI agents in Virginia and he is singing like a canary," POTUS said with a raised voice.

"Your tone and accusations are very insulting, Mr. President. I will leave you now." The call abruptly ended.

"Did he just hang up on me?" POTUS asked in bewilderment.

"It appears so, Sir, or the line could have been disconnected by accident," Wentworth said politely.

"Oh bullshit, Chuck! Stop blowing smoke," POTUS yelled. "That little shit just hung up on the President of the United States. Can I get an assessment of this call from all you so-called experts?"

Keenan was first to offer an opinion. "Sir, my assessment is that Jiang may be completely unaware that his Ministry of State Security has this information. If his lifelong friend Gao Zheng, who is the Head of State Security, unilaterally made the decision to hide the plot information from the United States, it would make sense for him to keep President Jiang in the dark in order to protect him."

"So, this phone call was a giant waste of time?" POTUS shot back.

"On the contrary, Sir," Keenan continued. "My hunch is that President Jiang is at this moment summoning Gao and his other boyhood friend Premier Li Wan to find out what's going on," Keenan added. "They were likely both listening in on the phone call just now. Jiang will sit them down and demand the truth. The question is, what will Jiang do if they tell him the truth?"

"What do you mean, Jim?" asked Wentworth.

"The Chinese are a formal bunch. They have deeply held convictions about saving face. If President Jiang is told there has been a cover-up of information, he won't just call us back and tell us that he was wrong and we were right. It would be far too embarrassing for him and for his government."

"So, what do we do?" Wentworth asked.

"Assuming Gao admits to a coverup, we need a way for President Jiang to tell us what he knows while still allowing him to save face," Keenan concluded.

"We don't have time for these games!" POTUS exploded.

The door to the Oval Office suddenly burst open without a knock, and Brian Howe, head of the President's Secret Service detail, rushed in. The Presidential helicopter Marine One could be seen landing on the White House lawn just outside. "Sir, we need to get you to a safe location immediately. We believe the White House is now a potential target."

"Where are we going?" POTUS asked, looking annoyed.

"Sir, we're flying out to Offutt Airforce Base in Omaha, Nebraska," Howe replied as he began escorting the President out to the lawn.

With Marine One's departure, CNN went to Breaking News, reporting that the President was being evacuated to a secure bunker in an undisclosed location by the Secret Service. They also reported that the Department of Homeland Security was initiating the Continuity of Government plan and moving key Congressional leadership to secure locations as well.

With the help of leaks from senior administration officials inside the White House, media outlets began to connect the dots on the stolen nuclear weapons in Iran with the threat of an Al-Qaeda attack on the United States. A heated barrage of questions pelted Kim Blazer, who stood alone at the podium of the White House press briefing room. Blazer deflected questions and spun her answers as best she could.

★★★

In Beijing, President Jiang tried to calm himself after hanging up on the President of the United States. He called his secretary, Ms. Chen, into his office. She had taken notes on the entire call. "I need to see Premier Li and Gao Zheng immediately. And have my son Peng join as well."

"Yes, Sir," she replied with a nod.

"Oh, and Ms. Chen, from your experience with the Americans, what does it mean to *sing like a canary*?" the President inquired.

"Sir, it means that Firefly is now in FBI custody, and he is telling the Americans everything he knows about the work he's done for us at the Ministry of State Security," she dutifully replied. "Ta ma de," the President whispered under his breath. *Fucking shit.*

COVERUP

CHAPTER 26

Qinzheng Hall, Office of the President: Beijing

After listening in on the phone call from the American President, Premier Li, Gao Zheng, and Jiang Peng arrived at Qinzheng Hall, the sprawling office of China's President. They had been summoned individually, and it was a surprise to all three men when they arrived together in the main lobby. Li and Gao exchanged quiet glances, silently reassuring one another that they would hold firm on keeping their important secret from the President. They were both curious as to why Jiang Peng had been invited to join the meeting and were unsure how he would react to his father's questioning.

Escorted into the office by the President's secretary, the three men sat facing one another in large, overstuffed seats positioned around a square coffee table.

President Jiang entered the room from his study, just off the main office. The three men stood in respect as he entered. The boyhood friends who were now the most powerful men in China smiled at one another and shook hands. The President then hugged his son and motioned for everyone to take their seats.

"Gentlemen, that was quite a phone call from the American President," the Chinese leader began. "As you know, the U.S. is bracing for an imminent, large-scale terrorist attack. The news media are now reporting it could involve nuclear weapons that have apparently been stolen from Iran."

The three men nodded in silence.

"Blakely claims we have information about this attack, and he is accusing this Government of covering it up," the President continued. "He claims that details of the plot were given to Firefly in Hong Kong. How is it that the American president knows our internal code name for Henry Kwok?"

The three men sat in an uncomfortable silence.

"We've known each other for a very long time," the President said, looking directly at Li and Gao. "So, I am going to ask you one time, and I want a straight answer. Did the Ministry of State Security know about this terrorist plot in advance, and does anyone in this government have the information that the Americans claim we have?"

"No, Mr. President," Li and Gao responded in almost perfect unison while Peng sat quietly.

"The Americans claim that Firefly is sitting with the FBI in the United States right now telling them everything he knows about the work he's done for us. I thought Firefly was working in Hong Kong?"

Gao and Li glanced at one another while Peng looked down at his shoes.

"We're trying to confirm the whereabouts of Firefly now," Gao began. "We believe he may have been sent to the United States by his employer in Hong Kong. We can't seem to locate Firefly's wife and children, either," Gao added.

The President continued, "This situation is critical. All U.S. airspace has been shut down. All international flights into the U.S. have been diverted in anticipation of a nuclear attack. And we just learned the American President is being relocated to a secure bunker," President Jiang went on. "The fact that the Americans believe we're hiding information that could potentially prevent this attack is not a good position for us to be in."

Peng's mind raced in nervous agitation. *How can my uncles sit here and lie to the President of China?* Peng understood that keeping his father out of the loop was ultimately for his own protection and for the good of the country. But his thoughts turned to the fate of millions of innocent Americans. *The U.S. doesn't know where to look. They should be searching for weapons on ships, not on airplanes!* The consequences of not warning the United States were too much to fathom. The prospect weighed heavily on Peng's conscience. If this coverup was ever proven, retaliation by the United States against China would be catastrophic: A war with America was unthinkable. He was distracted by his own thoughts, ignoring the conversation that was taking place in front of him.

"Peng? Are you alright?" the President inquired, noticing his son's distant stare.

"I'm feeling a little under the weather," the young man said, excusing himself for a bathroom break. He entered the private washroom and splashed cold water on his face. Staring at himself in the mirror, his mind churned for a solution. *How can I communicate what I know to the Americans without jeopardizing my father or my country?*

He needed a plan—and he needed one fast.

★★★

White House Communications Director Kim Blazer paced back and forth across her small West Wing office, in emotional distress after hearing the President's address to the nation. A petite thirty-year-old with a husband and three young children, she was deeply concerned that by not disclosing the nuclear threat to the public, the President was ignoring his responsibility to defend and protect the country. A devout Catholic, she was trained in feelings of guilt. She had fought unsuccessfully with speechwriters and the NSA over the lack of transparency in the POTUS address. It was the President's decision not to inform the public on the severity of the threat. Blazer considered that decision to be a case of sinful, gross negligence.

Keenan was right, she thought. *We're facing a nuclear disaster but giving the American public what amounts to a traffic alert. The public needs to know the truth, so they can prepare as best they can and make their peace. What we're doing is criminal.*

She picked up the phone and called her good friend Hester Blum, Executive Producer at Reuters News Agency, and told her everything. Thirty minutes later, television networks around the world went to "Breaking News," citing a Senior White House official: the imminent Al-Qaeda terrorist plot against the United States was likely to be nuclear in nature.

Across the U.S., shock turned to panic, and panic turned to unbridled pandemonium as Americans struggled to prepare for an attack that held little chance of survival.

Blazer followed the news coverage late into the evening from her West Wing office television:

> ***A Fox News Alert*** *– Looting and panic continued to escalate in cities across the nation this evening as news of a potential nuclear attack spread. The Governors of New York and California called out the National Guard to keep order, and they are imposing martial law effective at midnight. On Wall Street, markets are expected to remain closed with news that the President has now been moved to an undisclosed location.*

★★★

MV Copenhagen: Pacific Ocean: Speed 15 KTS

The *Copenhagen* was still in international waters, two hundred and seventy miles off the Coast of California. It was steaming in calm seas toward the approach channel to the Port of Los Angeles. Everything was on schedule. The ship would arrive in L.A. in a matter of hours. Captain Lars Anderson called his brother Neil who lived in Colorado and wished him a happy birthday before beginning preparations for docking in California.

"Lots going on in the U.S." his brother said. "Have you seen the latest news?"

★★★

MV Dresden: Panama Canal

Captain Hedger slowed the *Dresden* to just a few knots, allowing a tugboat from the Panama Canal Authority to join his ship alongside. The crew was careful in transferring the canal pilot from the tugboat onto the *Dresden* via the gangway stairs, which dangled off the side of the ship's hull. The pilot proceeded to the ship's bridge to begin the delicate process of bringing the *Dresden* through the locks of the Panama Canal and into Gatun Lake.

Hedger greeted the pilot and handed him control of the ship for the passage into the first lock.

"Sir, there are reports on the news wire that a terrorist attack may occur in the United States," his first officer announced.

"Well, I hope that's not the case. But we should be safe here in Panama," Hedger replied.

From the jungle hills approximately one mile from the Canal, an Al-Qaeda recruit sat waiting in the woods with a cell phone, binoculars, and $1,000 in cash he had been paid for conducting the mission. His instructions were simple. Wait for the *Dresden* to enter the first lock and then call the phone number that had been pre-programmed into his phone.

What the unfortunate recruit had not been told was that his phone call would trigger a nuclear explosion, and that he would never get the chance to spend the money. The ship, the locks, and everything within a five-mile radius would be instantly vaporized.

CONSCIENCE

CHAPTER 27

China's Ministry of State Security, Beijing

Jiang Peng was visibly distraught walking back to his office at the Ministry of State Security. Tormented by a growing sense of outrage and culpability, he sat at his desk until well after midnight watching CCTV coverage of the crisis unfold in the United States.

The Americans don't deserve this. My father doesn't deserve this.

He fidgeted in his seat and sipped a mug of green tea that had long since turned cold.

In his office safe, just a few feet away from his desk, sat all the information the Americans needed to know to avoid a catastrophe: the names of the cargo ships, the ID numbers of the two containers carrying *Romeo* and *Juliet*, as well as Al-Qaeda's intended targets. This was dangerous evidence. Proof that China could have prevented the deaths of a million innocent people. Proof that would leave a hideous stain on The People's Republic of China, a stain that his father would wear for all eternity.

How do I get this information to the Americans without implicating Beijing?

Peng felt light-headed from a lack of food, and he struggled to stay calm. He looked with pride at his diplomas, which were prominently displayed on his office wall: Milton Academy, The Army Defense School, and MIT. He gazed for a long moment at his Milton Academy diploma, reflecting fondly on his memorable teenage years in America and recalling the friendship and hospitality the Americans had shown him. Embossed in the middle of the Milton diploma was the school's official seal and the Academy's motto, "Dare to be True." As he read it aloud, he was suddenly struck by an overwhelming moment of clarity. He had an idea that just might work. *Jim Keenan,* he thought. *If I can quietly get a message to Jim that they need to search ships instead of airplanes, he will know what to do. He will understand the sensitivity of my situation. But how?*

Peng's mind raced as he stepped over to the office shelves containing his old textbooks. His eye was drawn to one in particular: *A History of the American Revolution.* It was a favorite from his school days in Massachusetts, where so much of the American Revolution had fomented. It was a book that he and Jim had dissected many times in their History Club discussions.

He took the book off the shelf and began thumbing through its pages. As he slowly closed the book, the illustration on the front cover caught his attention—a black and white drawing of Boston's Old North Church with two bright yellow lanterns hanging in the steeple. He recalled the simple code the Patriots had devised to warn the citizens of Boston about the invading British troops. One lantern would be hung if the British were coming by land, two lanterns if by sea. And it was two lanterns that night in Boston's Old North Church that launched Paul Revere on his legendary ride into the annals of American history.

"Two if by sea…" he whispered.

"Two if by sea…" he said louder with a burst of enthusiasm.

I can text this picture over to Jim. He will know the meaning of the two lanterns in the steeple and quickly piece together why I sent it. It was a simple code that conveyed a crucial message. The Al-Qaeda attacks on the U.S. were coming by ship, not by plane.

Peng quickly grabbed his mobile phone camera and took a photo of The Old North Church on the book's cover. At the bottom of the picture, he wrote: ACT QUICKLY, PAUL REVERE. He attached the photo to a text message using a double encrypted app called SIGNAL. After taking a deep breath, he hit "Send."

★★★

The West Wing was filled with noise and commotion while the continuity of government plan was being carried out. Agents Keenan and Bowman were still in the situation room awaiting word on which helicopter they needed to be on and which bunker they would be taken to. Sandwiches and salads had been sent in by the White House cafeteria.

Picking up a fork, Keenan suddenly heard his phone ping. It was a message coming in on his SIGNAL app, which narrowed the list of possible senders.

The message was from *Milton03*. It was Jiang Peng. He opened the text and was surprised to see a picture with the words "ACT QUICKLY, PAUL REVERE" underneath it.

Keenan immediately recognized Boston's Old North Church but struggled to recall where he had seen the image before. This was clearly a code of some sort from his friend Peng, and he pondered its meaning.

"What's the matter?" Laura asked, looking up from her salad.

"It's a text message from a very important friend," he answered, showing her the photo on his phone. "Two lanterns in Boston's Old North Church," he went on.

"Two if by sea," Laura interjected before taking a sip of water.

"Yes," Keenan replied, pleased that Laura knew her American history. He sat staring for a moment at the photo and at the message beneath. "Oh shit!" His voice projected across the room. Others seated near them looked over in his direction.

"What is it?" Laura asked, her face showing genuine concern.

"This is a picture from a book cover, *A History of the American Revolution*. It's one of my favorite books from high school. The only person who knows that is my roommate from Milton."

"I'm not following, Jim. What does this have to do with anything?"

Jim's face was animated, but he kept his voice low. "My boarding school roommate Jiang Peng came from a wealthy family in China. His father is the President of China."

"You roomed with President Jiang's son?" Laura asked, incredulous.

"Yes," Jim shot back. "He's a rising star in the Communist Party and is slated to take over China's Ministry of State Security someday—and maybe even become China's President down the road. We send occasional messages via SIGNAL, and *Milton03* is his text address."

Laura shook her head. "Okay, but I'm still not sure what this means."

James took a moment to gather his thoughts. "We know from Henry Kwok that Beijing is hiding information about an attack, right?"

"Yes."

We saw that information being passed to Kwok from the Iraqi agent in Hong Kong, and Kwok confirmed he gave it to his MSS handler Panda, which you witnessed and photographed at the Foreign Correspondents Club, right?"

"True."

"So, Beijing has the information, but for some reason they decided not to warn the United States. That means a faction in Beijing wants the attack on the U.S. to happen, probably the Ministry of State Security, to help fast track

China's own global ambitions. Peng is a high-level insider who works directly for Gao Zheng, the head of MSS. Peng is trying to tell us what he knows about the attack without allowing his father to lose face.

"Two if by SEA," Laura said aloud, seeing how the pieces fit together. "The attack isn't coming by airplane," she said. "It's coming by ship!"

"Exactly!" Jim replied. "We've been looking in all the wrong places."

★★★

MV Dresden: Panama Canal

As the *Dresden* sailed from the Gulf of Panama into the Cocoli Locks, Captain Hedger went onto the flyway extension just outside the ship's air-conditioned bridge to monitor progress. The Panamanian weather was oppressively hot and humid, but the outside flyway provided the best view of ship operations. The trip through the canal system would take about eleven hours with a transit fee of just over $1 million. Hedger marveled at the Canal's ingenuity. It was the engineering feat of its day and the dream of seafarers dating back to Columbus—a way to avoid the 8,000-nautical-mile voyage around the tip of South America.

Ferdinand de Lesseps had begun the canal project in the 1880s after successful construction of the Suez Canal. But Panama proved to be far more complicated and challenging. The project was a massive undertaking in the middle of a dense jungle. Malaria and yellow fever killed over 22,000 workers. After de Lesseps went bankrupt in 1889, the Americans took over construction, completing the fifty-one-mile Canal in 1914. Hedger watched as water rushed in around his ship, raising the vessel upward inside the lock using basic fluid dynamics. He never got tired of watching the process.

In the lush green hills off the ship's starboard side, the young Al-Qaeda recruit squinted into his binoculars for confirmation of the ship's identity as it floated inside the Cocoli Locks. The name *DRESDEN* was clearly visible, painted in bright white letters across the ship's black hull near the bow. The young recruit had been sitting in the heat and humidity for hours and couldn't wait to get back to town for a shower and to spend some of his bonus.

Reaching into his backpack, he took out the iPhone he had been given and pressed the side buttons to turn the phone on. It didn't work.

"The damn battery's dead," he whispered.

He took out the portable charger he had been given and plugged it into the phone. "Should work now," he said to himself as the white Apple logo suddenly appeared in the middle of the screen. He went to the iPhone's contact section and accessed the only phone number that had been stored there. It began with +92, which was the country code for Pakistan. He wondered for a moment why anyone would pay him $1000 just to place a phone call to Pakistan from the jungle. It didn't matter. The money was secure in his pocket. He touched the phone number highlighted in blue on his screen to activate the call. Gazing out at the *Dresden*, he put the phone to his ear and waited for a ring tone. He never knew what hit him.

The phone signal activated *Juliet's* triggering device, setting off a 25-kiloton fission chain reaction. The explosion blasted outward in a brilliant flash of a thousand suns. The fireball instantly expanded eight football fields in diameter, vaporizing everything within it, before rising into the air as a giant mushroom cloud that became visible across the Panamanian Isthmus.

The container ship *Hyundai Glory* was sitting sixty nautical miles from the Canal in the Gulf of Panama. The captain and crew on the bridge watched in shock as the giant mushroom cloud rose ominously into the late afternoon sky. The captain radioed his North American Headquarters in New York. "It appears there's been some kind of catastrophic explosion in the Panama Canal," the captain said urgently. "Request authorization to change course to Los Angeles."

As Keenan and Bowman contemplated the best response to the text message from Peng, everyone in the room was suddenly drawn to the television screens mounted on the Sit Room's walls. A staff member managed to find the right button on the TV control panel and turned up the volume.

"We Have CNN BREAKING NEWS from Panama."

> "Officials in Central America have just confirmed a massive explosion took place

> approximately thirty minutes ago inside the Panama Canal Zone. Officials report a large mushroom cloud rising over the Pacific side of the Canal near the Cocoli Locks. It is not clear at this time whether a ship has exploded. The U.S. Geological Survey confirms an 8.3 magnitude event registered on the Richter scale in that area. Stay tuned to CNN Breaking News for details."

"Oh no!" Keenan gasped, grabbing Laura's hand. His cell phone rang—it was Tom Fahey.

"Tom, our friend in Beijing just sent me a coded message telling us that the attacks are coming by ship, not by airplane. Are you watching the news?"

"Get packed, Jim. We're being evacuated to Raven Rock. Meet me on the lawn in fifteen minutes. You can fill me in there."

Laura Bowman's phone pinged at the same time with a text message from her boss Richard Holmes. Quickly reading it, she said tightly, "Looks like we're all going to Raven Rock."

SCRAMBLE

CHAPTER 28

The White House Ellipse

"Tom, the explosion in the Canal had to be a cargo ship! We've got to shut down the ports NOW!" Keenan yelled toward Fahey as they ran to the rendezvous point on the southside of the White House called the Ellipse.

"Panama's gone, Jim. I mean it's fucking gone! Can you believe this shit?" Fahey asked, running a hand through the top of his hair.

"Tom, we've been looking in the wrong place. The bombs are on ships, probably inside shipping containers. The attack is by sea!"

"Start from the beginning and tell us what you have," Fahey said, staring at his friend.

"The explosion had to be a cargo ship. Just before the explosion, I received a text message from our friend Jiang Peng in Beijing."

"Your Milton roommate?" Wentworth asked.

"Yes, Sir. He's high level at China's MSS. He texted me this picture," Keenan said, showing both men his iPhone screen. "It's the Old North Church in Boston with two lanterns shining in the steeple, and it's signed Paul Revere," Keenan explained.

"Two if by sea," Fahey blurted out.

"Yes. Exactly!"

"That's pretty clever," Wentworth added, his expression brightening.

"Yes, Sir. And besides telling us the attacks are coming by ship, this message is full of other critical information. It tells us that China's Ministry of State Security does in fact have the information President Jiang denied having, which means that President Jiang has likely been kept in the dark on what's going on. This coverup is being orchestrated by the President's inner circle. It implicates China's Ministry of State Security head Gao Zheng and maybe his good friend Premier Li as well. This confirms that a conscious decision was made by a faction inside China's leadership to hide information from the United States that could impact our national security," Keenan concluded.

"They see an opportunity in having the United States pivot back to the Middle East," Wentworth said, shaking his head.

"Yes, Sir."

"That puts Jiang Peng in a very precarious situation," Fahey added. "He's been allowed access to critical attack intelligence, and he could be killed for leaking it to us."

"We need to protect this guy, Tom," Keenan insisted.

"First, we have to alert the President and start searching ships," Wentworth interjected.

"The President needs to authorize Ben Halsey at DHS to work with Customs and Border Patrol to close all shipping ports immediately," Fahey advised Wentworth. "The Coast Guard and Navy also require his authorization to begin boarding vessels with nuke sniffers right away."

Wentworth was already dialing his mobile phone. He reached Chris Dodd, the President's Chief of Staff, who was with POTUS aboard the Boeing 747 Airborne Operations Center. It was a specially designed jumbo jet that could be refueled and remain in the air indefinitely, allowing the President to run the government while keeping him safe from a nuclear blast.

"This is Wentworth, Chris. I need to speak with the President."

"What do we have, Chuck?" the President's voice suddenly sounded on the call.

Wentworth quickly briefed POTUS about the Panama blast and the cryptic message received from China.

"Ben Halsey is on the plane with me, Chuck, and he's listening in," POTUS replied. "We'll get our forces redirected to ships and ports immediately. I've initiated COGCON 1 to scramble key leadership into secure bunkers, and the Shadow Government protocol is activated."

"Yes, Sir," Wentworth answered. "We're at the Ellipse now, boarding evacuation helicopters."

"Good to hear, Chuck. Talk soon." The call ended.

"POTUS and Halsey are together on the Air Ops 747," Wentworth informed the group. "They're shifting the focus of the bomb search to cargo ships and ports right away."

"Excellent," Fahey said.

Three CH-47 Chinook helicopters gently hovered just above the Ellipse before settling onto the south side of the White House as VIP passengers waited for the all-clear to board.

"Where is this place we're going to?" Laura asked, standing next to Keenan.

"Raven Rock Mountain Complex," Keenan yelled above the chopper's rotor noise. "It's a bunker near Blue Ridge Summit, Pennsylvania," he continued. "We call it the underground Pentagon. It works together with the Emergency Operations Center in Virginia and the Cheyenne Mountain Complex in Colorado."

Dust whipped around the chopper rotors as government leaders were escorted in pre-assigned groups to their respective flights. The Speaker of the House climbed into the first copter with the Senate Majority Leader, the Secretary of the Treasury, and the U.S. Attorney General. The Secretaries of the Interior, Agriculture, and Commerce along with the President Pro Tempore of the Senate boarded the second chopper.

Wentworth, Fahey, and FBI Director Susan Kendall along with Keenan, Bowman, and Holmes boarded the third helicopter and donned their green David Clark headsets.

"The Vice President has been moved to the Mount Weather Bunker in Virginia," Wentworth said into his microphone, reading from his incoming texts. "The Secretary of State is safe in Israel, and the Secretary of Defense is already at Raven Rock," he concluded.

"It looks like we're really going to get hit," Fahey added over the noise of the whirling rotor blades.

With everyone aboard, the three Chinooks roared to full power and slowly lifted off before flying out in different directions.

Keenan reached over and gently squeezed Laura's knee in a weak attempt at reassurance.

As they flew low above the capital rooftops, Laura stared out the window, once again sensing her father's calming presence. She put her hand on Jim's, not caring if anyone noticed. Closing her eyes, she took a deep breath and allowed her thoughts to drift longingly back to Hong Kong.

SIGNALS

CHAPTER 29

Raven Rock Mountain Complex, Blue Ridge Summit, Pennsylvania

The team exited their chopper and headed deep into the Raven Rock complex. They proceeded to the bunker's control center, affectionately known as *The Tank*, for a situation briefing. A multitude of video screens filled the massive center, broadcasting a network of government and military leaders from various secure locations. POTUS and Halsey were on a live feed from 40,000 feet aboard the Air Ops 747.

Halsey was anxious to begin the briefing.

"Mr. President, FEMA has implemented NATIONAL RESPONSE 1, which means all U.S. citizens are now receiving text messages with instructions on duck and cover techniques and other precautionary blast measures. We've shut down all maritime traffic in and around the United States coastline. The Navy together with the Coast

Guard have now been authorized to board and investigate all cargo vessels in U.S. waters. We are having issues finding enough nuke sniffing technology to deploy."

"Ben, I think it's important you fill everyone in on just how daunting this search will be," POTUS chimed in.

"Well folks, the United States has 88,633 miles of shoreline, and there are approximately 50,000 merchant marine ships at sea around the world at any given time. The United States imports thirty million cargo containers from around the world each year. Less than five percent of those containers are ever physically inspected."

"How are we addressing the scale of this search, Ben?" POTUS asked.

"Sir, we've got our best and brightest working on it. We're running Bayes."

"Bayes?" Chief of Staff Dobbs asked.

"Bayesian Search Theory," Halsey explained. "It's a mathematical formula used to calculate conditional probabilities. It was initially developed to find a hydrogen bomb that was lost off the coast of Spain in 1966. The Navy also used it to find the USS Scorpio submarine in 1968, which was 2600 miles out in the Atlantic Ocean under 10,000 feet of water. They found the sub just 200 yards from where the math said it would be. More recently it's been used to locate missing airplanes, like that Malaysian Airliner. Our people are using it to try and narrow down the search for high-risk containers onboard suspicious ships."

"And what are our chances of finding these things before they detonate?" POTUS asked.

"Sir, to be frank" Halsey continued, "without any additional information, this will be like trying to find my contact lenses in the middle of the Pacific Ocean."

The silence at Raven Rock was deafening. Fahey got up and pulled Wentworth, Keenan, and Holmes over for a sidebar conversation.

"Jim, your friend Jiang Peng took a substantial risk by sending you this coded message. Would he do it again?"

"The problem, Tom, is how to communicate with Peng," Keenan explained. "The Chinese are monitoring most text message apps. I'm sure they are monitoring government texts. They like catching high level officials chatting with their girlfriends to use as leverage later. That's why Peng texted me a picture instead of using words. Nobody in China would know what that picture means if it were intercepted. And he used the SIGNAL messaging app which is double encrypted and much more secure than their WeChat system."

"What if you sent him a picture back? Some recognizable meeting place in his area with a meeting time under it. Our Beijing team can organize a brush pass with Peng and get all the information we need without putting him at risk from electronic communications," Fahey replied.

"It's worth a shot, Jim," Wentworth chimed in.

"It's 0700 hours in the morning in Beijing. If we act now, we could have the information from Peng by midnight our time. That is, if he really wants to help us," Fahey said.

The Monument to the People's Heroes, a ten-story obelisk statue in the middle of Tiananmen Square, popped into Keenan's head. He Googled a photo of it.

The square will be crowded with people at this time of the morning, a good place for a handoff, he thought. Jim attached a photo of the monument to Peng's original text and put a string of bold capital letters underneath the picture: **MDDC-HMSDK-0900.** Then he hit "Send."

"We need to have our Beijing guys prepare to meet Peng at the People's Hero Monument at 0900 hours their time," Keenan told the team. "That gives him two hours. If he receives this text and can help us further, he will find a way to be there."

Wentworth immediately got on the phone with Ambassador Bowlen in Beijing.

Keenan and Fahey called CIA Station Chief Ken Barrow and told him everything he would need to set up the meet.

"What do the letters mean under the picture you sent Peng?" Laura asked.

"It's a crude kids code, but it's all I could think of. Peng's favorite movie in high school was *2001 A Space Odyssey.* He loved how Stanley Kubrick named the evil computer HAL, which was really code for IBM.

"What do you mean?" Laura asked.

"You go up to the next letter in the word HAL, so the H becomes **I**, the A becomes **B**, and the L becomes **M.** HAL becomes IBM. Peng will translate MDDC-HMSDK-0900 into NEED-INTEL-9AM and match that up with the monument picture in Tiananmen Square as the rendezvous point."

"You're sure he will figure all that out?"

"I'm very sure."

With phone calls made and the plan in place, the team turned briefly to catch the latest news:

CNN Breaking News:

"CNN can confirm that the bomb that exploded in the Panama Canal today was on board the MV Dresden, a large container ship that was transiting the Canal enroute to New York. The ship was inside the Cocoli Locks when the detonation occurred. The Pentagon estimates the blast came from a nuclear weapon with a yield of twenty-five kilotons. The bomb dropped on Hiroshima was fifteen kilotons in strength. At this hour, an international rescue operation is underway. It is not known if the United States is part of the rescue effort. The Federal Emergency Management Agency is warning all U.S. Citizens to stay indoors and preferably in concrete basements where available. The President of the United States has been moved to an undisclosed location along with the Cabinet and Congressional leadership as part of the Continuity of Government protocol. Stay tuned to CNN for continuous coverage."

★★★

At the Port of Los Angeles, the *Copenhagen* had completed its operations, successfully offloading its containers onto cargo trucks for onward delivery. Captain Anderson was eager to get underway for the next port of call in Vancouver. Container ICLU265298, which had *Romeo* inside, was picked up at the Port by Eagle Transport Trucking. The truck and container passed through the Port's security gate and headed north toward downtown Los Angeles. Eagle Transport had unwittingly hired an Al-Qaeda recruit named Jamal just a week prior without any background check. The truck driver shortage in Los Angeles put potential new hires on a fast track to getting behind the wheel. Jamal's instructions from Al-Qaeda were clear: Pull the truck over on Figueroa Street at the address indicated and call the pre-programmed number on the cell phone he had been given.

As he headed northbound on the 110 Freeway, Jamal could see hundreds of police and military vehicles with sirens blaring and lights flashing all speeding in the opposite direction toward the Port. The sky overhead was dotted with police helicopters, news helicopters, and aerial drones.

Glad I got out of there before all that shit started, he thought. As a new recruit for Al-Qaeda, he wanted to make a good first impression by getting the truck to its destination without any delays. He had been paid a $1000 cash bonus for his first assignment, and he needed to pay his rent.

BRUSH PASS

CHAPTER 30

Ministry of State Security, Beijing

Jiang Peng's phone vibrated with an incoming text from USNA07—it was Jim Keenan. He nervously opened the message and gazed at the picture, instantly recognizing the Monument to the People's Heroes in Tiananmen Square.

Peng translated the coded letters underneath the picture. It was 07:10, and Tiananmen Square was close by his office. He could easily get to the rendezvous location by 09:00. He typed out the most critical information he knew about the Al-Qaeda attack on his laptop, but before printing a copy, he suddenly paused.

Peng was a highly intelligent man but did not consider himself to be an intellectual. He tried as best he could to live by the Confucian virtues of benevolence, righteousness, and fidelity, which he did through hard work, fair play, and responsible leadership. As he sat staring at his computer screen, he wondered if there might still be a way to reset China's relationship with the United States after this unnecessary debacle. A way to send the Americans a clear message that China's old guard was being replaced by a new generation of leaders interested in a more collaborative approach between the United States and China rather than a zero-sum game. Thinking hard on what he was about to do, Peng took an honest inventory of his motives and decided it was time to put all the chips on the table.

The Americans had captured Henry Kwok, but he was just a pawn in an elaborate web of high-level espionage and treason. To reveal China's true double agent inside the CIA would expose the most valuable spy the Ministry of State Security had ever known. But he knew that as long as this type of intrigue and betrayal continued, there could never be a level of trust between Washington and Beijing, and there would always remain an existential threat to everything China hoped to accomplish. Peng looked back at his computer screen and decided to type one additional line of information in bold letters for the Americans. A shocking revelation that would hopefully be received as it was intended. As an honest gesture of good will. Peng printed out a copy of his message, deleted the file, and headed out for Tiananmen Square.

Agent Ken Barrow sent the best he had for the meeting with Jiang Peng. Ellen Tso was a career CIA officer and an expert in spycraft. She was briefed and shown several photographs of Peng. The briefing wasn't necessary. She had been studying the Ministry of State Security's leadership for months and knew everything there was to know about the President's son.

Tso headed out for Tiananmen Square. She took two taxis to avoid being followed and changed her hat and sunglasses for good measure. Arriving at the Monument of the People's Heroes at 8:45, she began slowly walking around the statue in a clockwise direction, scanning the crowd, hoping to make contact.

Jiang Peng arrived at the Monument at 08:55 and began slowly walking around it counterclockwise, guessing correctly that his contact would be circling the other way. Tso recognized Peng on their first pass. She looked him in the eye and gave an almost indiscernible nod, unsure what would happen next. On their second pass, Peng turned suddenly and walked in the same direction as Tso. At a natural pace, he caught up to her from behind and gently slipped a folded paper into the left pocket of her blazer. With the pass complete, they each turned and walked in opposite directions, leaving the square unnoticed.

Tso hurried to a taxi and returned to Ken Barrow's office at the U.S. Embassy. She handed Barrow the folded paper from Jiang, and he began to read:

- *Confirm this is an Al-Qaeda Operation: 2 X Fission Nuclear Devices sent on two SHIPS*
- *Bombs Sailed from Bandar Abbas / Transloaded in Shanghai for the USA*

- *Weapon JULIET, on MV DRESDEN, Container# ICLU2236677, Exploded - PANAMA CANAL*
- *Weapon ROMEO, on MV COPENHAGEN, Container# ICLU265298, Target – LOS ANGELES*
- *Weapons have Cell Phone triggering devices*
- *L.A. Container Destination - MEDTEC on Figueroa Street, LA*
- *Nuke's origin is IRAN (weapons were not stolen)*
- ***THOMAS FAHEY IS WORKING FOR MSS IN BEIJING***

P. REVERE

"Did you read any of this material, Ellen?" Barrow asked.

"No, Sir. I was not instructed to read it," she replied, worried by Barrow's alarmed facial expression.

"Thank you, Ellen. Great work. I'll take it from here."

As Tso left his office, Ken Barrow stared in disbelief at the message from Jiang Peng.

Tom Fahey is a fucking mole?

It was too much to comprehend, and at the same time he had to communicate Jiang's note to Wentworth and Keenan urgently. There was no time for an embassy-secured communication. He sent the information to Keenan and Wentworth via WhatsApp but did not include the startling news about Tom Fahey.

Instead, he sent a separate text message to Richard Holmes and Laura Bowman, warning of the tragic revelation. As senior counterintelligence agents sitting inside

Raven Rock, it would be up to them to manage the Fahey situation together with the ongoing crisis.

At Raven Rock, text message pings were sounding off constantly. Wentworth and Keenan received the urgent message from Ken Barrow. As they digested the message from Beijing together, Fahey wondered why he had been left off Barrow's text distribution. It was highly unusual, and he became noticeably suspicious and agitated.

"Let's get all hands on deck for a briefing right NOW," Wentworth shouted.

★★★

POTUS and Ben Halsey appeared on the largest TV monitor at Raven Rock while other key members of the leadership team flashed on smaller screens from their respective bunkers. This time it was Charles Wentworth who was anxious to begin the meeting.

"Sir, we've received new information from our credible Chinese source that Al-Qaeda's second target is Los Angeles. The second bomb is in a cargo container. We have the container number and the ship it's coming in on; that information has been relayed to DHS, DOD, Coast Guard, and the Navy."

"Sir, we're currently operating a search and destroy mission with the Navy Seals taking the lead," Defense Secretary Metcalf added.

"The intelligence from China confirms this is an Al-Qaeda attack and that the nukes came from Iran," Wentworth continued.

"Sir, we should notify the citizens of Los Angeles," FEMA Director Ted Ryan interjected.

"Ted, I'm scared to death the city of Los Angeles will come completely unglued," POTUS replied.

"But Sir, we have an obligation to warn the public if the threat is specific to a location," the FEMA director argued.

White House Communications Director Susan Blazer unblocked her video camera, and her concerned face suddenly appeared on one of the Center's screens.

POTUS continued, "Ted, go ahead and initiate a text warning to all area codes in Southern California advising that we have a credible terrorist threat that could be nuclear in nature. Susan, inform the media with the same information. Do NOT mention the use of shipping containers. Those damn things are everywhere. People will see them on the streets, and it will turn into a complete shit show. Secretary Halsey, go on the air with one of the major networks to remind everyone they should remain indoors and in basements where possible."

"Yes, Sir."

"Ladies and Gentlemen," the President continued in his most serious tone. "The Secretary of Defense, the Joint Chiefs, and the Department of Homeland Security are hereby authorized to take whatever action is necessary and to use whatever means possible to protect and defend our citizens. The American people are depending on us at this critical hour. Let's not let them down."

As the President finished issuing orders, several TV monitors inside Raven Rock and the other bunker locations switched to the Pentagon's live video feed of the military operations being conducted at the Port of Los Angeles. The video included communications between troop leaders and the operations command center.

"I can't believe America is going through this shit all over again," Keenan said, staring at the video monitors on the wall that looked like a remake of the Hollywood Squares. He looked around the control room but couldn't locate Laura or Richard Holmes.

In a briefing room just off the main control center, Bowman and Holmes stood behind closed doors trying to digest the text message from Ken Barrow. There was no proof to implicate Tom Fahey as a double agent other than the word of a high-level spy inside China's Ministry of State Security. That was all the reason anyone needed to carefully and methodically investigate Fahey, but it needed to be done quietly and in a manner that allowed for some semblance of presumed innocence. Laura thought of what the news would do to Jim. *It will be like killing his father all over again*, she thought.

Personnel inside Raven Rock began turning toward the TV monitors to catch the interview with DHS's Ben Halsey broadcasting live from the Air Ops 747:

FOX NEWS SPECIAL REPORT:

"The Department of Homeland Security is issuing a specific threat alert for the City of Los Angeles. Joining us by video feed is DHS Secretary Ben Halsey from an undisclosed location. Mr. Secretary, what can you tell us?"

"We are urging all citizens in and around the Los Angeles area to remain calm, to stay indoors, and to shelter in basements or concrete structures if possible. FEMA has sent a text message with these instructions to all area codes in Southern California."

"Mr. Secretary, is this a nuclear threat? Are we looking at something like Panama?"

"We can't be certain at this time, but given what just happened in Panama, it's reasonable to assume that the threat to Los Angeles is real and that we should be taking every precaution."

"Where is the President?"

"The President is safe. He is in a special control center that was built for this type of situation. He is overseeing all aspects of our response to this crisis."

"And the Vice President?"

"The Vice President is also safe and overseeing operations from a separate location. We will make further announcements as information becomes available."

"Thank you, Mr. Secretary. That was Department of Homeland Security Chief, Ben Halsey, talking to us live from what appeared to be an airplane."

PANIC

CHAPTER 31

Los Angeles, California

A nuclear threat warning for the City of Los Angeles was broadcast by news channels, social media outlets, and FEMA's text messaging system. Within moments, the population of more than four million people erupted into total chaos.

In a city known for crime, cultural tensions, and twenty-four-hour traffic jams, this was a horror scene even the most seasoned Californian could not have imagined. The 405 freeway along with the 5, 10, 101, and 110 Freeways stood in total gridlock as residents tried to escape north and east out of the L.A. basin. One news reporter noted that walking to Phoenix would be faster than driving, and with no public transit system to speak of, some decided to do just that.

In East L.A., looting and physical confrontations raged out of control. Inglewood parents ran with small children in their arms to the new SOFI football stadium, hoping the sheer size of the structure might provide protection. Residents of Hollywood, Brentwood, Bel-Air, and Malibu ignored the flight moratorium and raced to their private jets with stylists and nannies in tow. Many from California's infamous cult communities calmly made their way to the city's beaches with lounge chairs and blankets, contentedly prepared to witness the end of days. At the University of Southern California, thousands of stranded students rushed to Frat Row, determined to ring in the end of the world with the biggest party the school had ever seen.

From police helicopters high above the city, a sea of humanity scrambled in a thousand directions, like ants trying to avoid a poisonous can of pesticide. Mayor Alfonse Ginette tried to project calm, though it was clear he was broadcasting from the safety of his own secure bunker.

The Port of Los Angeles

From the bridge of the *Copenhagen*, Captain Anderson had a bird's eye view of the police and military onslaught rushing into the Port of L.A. SWAT teams, Army HUMV's, National Guard vehicles, and California State police poured through the terminal gates as military helicopters and F18 fighter jets buzzed overhead. It took several minutes for Anderson to realize that the invasion forces were heading directly toward his ship.

He turned to see a team of Navy Seals being lowered onto the *Copenhagen's* bridge by a large SH-60 Seahawk helicopter. The Seals entered the interior of the bridge, aiming their weapons squarely at Anderson and his XO Stephen Jensen, who both stood motionless in disbelief. Cameras on the Seal Team helmets broadcast the entire operation to Raven Rock and other government command locations.

"Get down on the floor, face down, and hands behind your back," came the order from the Seal Team commander. Anderson and his XO hit the deck. They were searched for weapons and then helped to a standing position facing the Seal team leader.

"Captain, there's a nuclear weapon in one of the containers you have aboard this ship. I need your manifest and the ship's stowage plan now," the Seal Commander yelled above the roar of chopper blades.

The XO pointed to the computer screen on the bridge console. They rushed over to it and brought up the manifest data.

"I'm looking for container ICLU265298. I need to know where it's stowed."

The XO made a handful of keystrokes into the system. "That container is no longer aboard the ship. It was discharged off the vessel about an hour ago to Eagle Transport Trucking. It's consigned to a company called MedTec on Figueroa Street, which I believe is in downtown Los Angeles," Jensen said rapidly.

"ALL UNITS, be advised the target container has been discharged from the vessel and is enroute to Figueroa Street via Eagle Transport Trucking," the Seal Commander shouted into his headset. "Repeat, Eagle Transport Trucking presumably heading to Figueroa."

The Commander turned to Captain Anderson. "Captain, there are a shitload of different color containers out there. Do you know what color this one would be?"

"This box will be either white or gray with the logo of a giant N painted on the side and the words *NORDIC* down the length of the box. The container number will be printed on top of the box so you can identify it from the air," Anderson said. "You know there are hundreds if not thousands of these containers all over this city," Anderson warned.

"Then we'll have to blow up every fucking one of them until we hit the box we're looking for," the Commander replied as he directed his team off the ship's bridge before turning back to Anderson.

"Captain, we can't be sure there's not another container bomb aboard this ship. You're to cut and run immediately and sail to these coordinates," he said, handing Anderson a printout. "Once you arrive at these coordinates, you'll be airlifted off the ship by helicopter along with your remaining crew."

"What then?" Anderson asked.

"Then we're going to blow this ship to kingdom come."

As the Seals departed, Anderson urgently prepared his ship and crew for an immediate departure out of Los Angeles.

"Get Nordic Lines HQ on the phone," he instructed Jensen. "They're not going to believe this one."

ZERO HOUR

CHAPTER 32

Downtown Los Angeles

Jamal steered his truck carrying the deadly cargo from San Pedro up the 110 Harbor Freeway toward downtown Los Angeles. The truck's radio blared breaking news and safety alerts from the emergency broadcasting system about the threat warning to Southern California. Still a few miles from the Figueroa Street exit, he unwrapped a sandwich from 7-Eleven and began to eat.

In the sky above, police and military helicopters barely missed one another as they crisscrossed the sunny California sky. Military jets flew wide sorties around the city and out over the Pacific coastline. Drones hovered above the freeway, monitoring motorists who had abandoned their vehicles in frustration and started to walk.

At Raven Rock, Bowman and Holmes took Director Charles Wentworth into a private briefing room. "We've got critical information that will be difficult for you to hear, Sir," Holmes began.

"What is it?" Wentworth asked.

"Sir, we've suspected," Laura Bowman began, "that Henry Kwok is not the only problem at the CIA. He's too low level. There is no way he could have accessed the names and phone numbers of our China assets on his own. Under normal circumstances he would have been fired for violating his disciplinary probation. Instead, he received numerous second chances before finally being let go."

"And?" Wentworth demanded tensely.

Holmes spoke next. "Sir, we received a tip from a highly credible source telling us who the real mole is," he paused. "There is no easy way to put this. The source claims the high-level mole at CIA is Tom Fahey."

Wentworth stared at Bowman, then at Holmes, and then back at Bowman, unable to speak. "Tom Fahey is one of the best agents this organization has ever had," Wentworth muttered.

"Yes, Sir."

"He has served this agency in multiple roles and in multiple countries for over thirty years. His father was a decorated CIA hero."

"We understand, Sir."

"He built the China desk at Langley into what it is today, the best group of intelligence analysts, technology experts, and spy assets anywhere in the clandestine service. He's spent the last decade providing Presidents and White

House administration officials with everything they need to know about what the Chinese are up to."

"Yes, Sir." Bowman and Holmes exchanged a look.

"So, who the hell is claiming that Tom Fahey is a fucking mole for China?"

"Sir, the news is coming *from* China. The source is Jiang Peng, the President's son."

★★★

Looking for a single shipping container in Los Angeles was like searching for a specific blade of grass in Central Park. Millions of cargo containers were imported and exported through Southern California every year. Some went to warehouses in the area while others were taken to railyards for onward distribution by train to the U.S. Midwest. From the air, cargo containers ubiquitously dotted the L.A. landscape for as far as the eye could see. The severe traffic jam across the city made it easier to isolate and identify containers on the ground, but their sheer number made the task laboriously slow.

Lieutenant Commander Blake Holloway from Seal Team Six was the designated mission leader. He communicated by radio from his chopper to the rest of his men in the air and on the ground. "Be advised we're targeting a gray or white cargo container with the word *NORDIC* printed on the sides. Our target container has the following identification number painted on top: India, Charlie, Lima, Uniform 265298," Holloway said into his headset microphone. "The delivery destination could be Figueroa Street," he said. "We need to look everywhere."

The plan was to deploy helicopters along a search area between the seaport and downtown L.A. Once the target container was identified, Seal Team commandos would converge on its location from the air with fighter jets in support.

"Raven Rock Center—Commander Holloway here, how do you read?"

"Loud and clear, Commander."

"Center, the search is progressing as planned. What are our orders once we've identified the target?"

Secretary of Defense Lindsey Metcalf was sitting inside Raven Rock asking herself the same question. It seemed logical to neutralize the target container by destroying it. But she was not sure if hitting the container with a missile could detonate the nuclear bomb inside.

"Lindsey?" the President queried over the intercom from the Air Ops 747. "What do we do when we find this thing?"

★★★

On the other side of Raven Rock, Wentworth was still being briefed on the news about Tom Fahey. "Given the source of the information, we have to treat this seriously," Wentworth said to Bowman and Holmes. "But it wouldn't be the first time an enemy has fed us misinformation about someone for their own benefit. We know Jiang Peng is a friend of Jim Keenan's, and he is trying to help us avoid an attack at great risk to himself. We have to assume this is credible intel, but why would a top China spy give up his most valuable asset?"

Laura asked, "What do you want us to do next, Sir?"

"We need to get Tom into a secure area—quietly. Take all forms of electronic communication from him and put a couple of our Marines in the room to guard him until we get beyond this crisis. Then we can investigate thoroughly."

"Will do," Laura answered briskly.

"And we need to inform Jim of the situation," Wentworth said with sadness.

"Sir, I can handle that if you'll allow," Bowman offered.

"Very well, Ms. Bowman. But inform him after we have Fahey secured. I don't want any drama playing out that would distract us during this crisis."

★★★

In the air over Los Angeles, Lieutenant Commander Holloway was still awaiting orders from Raven Rock Center.

"Stand by, Commander," Metcalf said.

"Mr. President, we need to get Colonel Dunn from Strategic Air Command on the line for some guidance on how to manage the bomb container once we find it."

"Just what we need," the President complained. "More happy thoughts from Colonel *All Dunn*."

Bowman and Holmes took three armed Marines who were part of the Raven Rock security detail to apprehend Fahey. They searched everywhere inside Raven Rock, including the restrooms and the storage areas. He was nowhere to be found. Tom Fahey had vanished.

★★★

"Colonel Dunn," POTUS said over the video network, "our Navy Seals are looking for a 25-kiloton nuclear weapon inside a shipping container near downtown Los Angeles. What do we do when we find it?"

"What do you mean, Mr. President?"

"What happens if our military neutralizes this container by blowing it up? Do we risk setting off a nuclear blast?" POTUS asked.

"That's a difficult question, Mr. President."

"And we need you to answer it, Colonel. A city with four million Americans hangs in the balance."

"Mr. President, nuclear weapons detonate high explosives to trigger a nuclear reaction. There have been cases of what we call "broken arrow" accidents involving nuclear weapons where the high explosive portion of the weapon has detonated without causing a nuclear explosion. For a nuclear blast to occur, explosives fire a bullet of Uranium 235 into a sphere that generates a fission reaction. The process must be very precise to work."

"Colonel Dunn, if we hit this container with a missile, are we going to accidentally blow up the City of Los Angeles? Yes, or no?" POTUS demanded.

"I can't answer that, Sir," Dunn replied. "I guess anything is possible."

★★★

Jamal and his truck finally reached Figueroa Street. As he exited the freeway, a Black Hawk helicopter appeared overhead. It hovered just above his truck as he pulled over in front of the Jonathan Club across the street from the Westin Bonaventure Hotel.

"We've got the target in sight," Lieutenant Commander Holloway bellowed into his headset. "Container identification number is a match. All units, gather on me at Figueroa," he advised the other Seal Team choppers in the vicinity.

"Raven Rock Center, we have the target in sight parked on Figueroa. What are our orders? Do we kill this thing or not?"

Military and government officials inside Raven Rock and across the Command Center communications network went silent, waiting to hear the President's order.

"Options, please, from my Joint Chiefs?" POTUS asked.

"We recommend blowing it up right now, Mr. President," General Alex Toomay, Chairman of the Joint Chiefs, said with confidence. "Low probability that this will be anything more than a localized explosion."

"And you're willing to take that chance, General?"

"Yes, Sir. We don't have any other options, and we need to act fast. The truck driver has most likely been recruited as a suicide bomber to detonate the nuke with his cell phone."

President Blakely paused, his mind churning through scenarios. History was full of bad advice given to Presidents by the military: Kennedy at the Bay of Pigs, Bush in Iraq.

"Commander Holloway, this is the President."

"Yes, Sir!"

"Can you put a missile through that truck's cab and kill the driver without blowing up the container?"

"Sir, we can put a missile straight up the driver's ass if that is your order. But I recommend using machine guns on the cab to keep the container intact."

Jamal looked up from his driver's side window. It was now obvious from the helicopter gunships hovering in the sky above that his truck was of special interest to the U.S. military. He knew what he had to do. He reached for his cell phone.

All Presidents experience it at some point during their term in office—a life or death decision that must be made all alone. *Success has many fathers, but failure is an orphan*, POTUS recalled President Kennedy saying after the Bay of Pigs disaster.

"Commander, you are authorized to take out the driver immediately," POTUS instructed.

Holloway's UH-60 Black Hawk helicopter suddenly appeared, hovering in front of Jamal's windshield.

The two men made eye contact, and Holloway could see the iPhone in Jamal's hand. He gave the Jihadist a wave goodbye as a second Black Hawk hovering directly above the truck opened fire with two .50 caliber Gatling machine gun cannons. The 1300-round-per minute barrage of gunfire straight down through the roof pulverized the truck and its driver into tiny, unrecognizable pieces.

"Driver is neutralized," Holloway reported.

"Commander, do we have a chopper that can lift that container and take it out to sea?" POTUS asked.

"Yes, Sir. My team can rig the box to a heavy lift chopper and fly it out of here."

"Commander, please proceed with that option," said POTUS.

The leadership team in the command center and on the video conference network sat in awe of the clear-headed ingenuity of the President. It was a display of *finest hour* leadership that no one had expected from him. They had just witnessed the brash and egotistical businessman from Alabama transform himself into a United States President.

★★★

A CH-47 Chinook heavy lift helicopter hovered above the Figueroa Street location while smoke billowed from the remains of Jamal and his truck. Seal Team commandos on the ground rigged heavy gauge lifting cables from the bottom of the chopper to the top four corners of the cargo container. Once secured, Holloway gave a thumb's up, and the Chinook engines roared, lifting the container off its chassis wheels and high into the air. With the container dangling beneath it, the Chinook turned south and flew straight out toward the Pacific Ocean.

The Raven Rock Command Center erupted in applause as live video showed the Chinook and the container flying away from the downtown area. As the celebration continued inside Raven Rock, Laura reluctantly approached Keenan. She gently put her hand on his shoulder. “I have some urgent and upsetting news, Jim. I need to talk to you right away. In private.”

PRECAUTIONS

CHAPTER 33

MV Copenhagen: Speed 25 knots

The *Copenhagen* was steaming full speed toward the coordinates assigned by the U.S. Navy. Captain Anderson and his crew were visibly on edge, wondering if they were unwitting passengers aboard a floating nuclear bomb.

A flotilla of naval vessels, Coast Guard cutters, and military aircraft escorted the ship to its final resting place. Anderson had been in contact with Nordic Lines Headquarters in Denmark and tried his best to explain why he was about to sink a $150 million ship on purpose. After years of safely navigating the world's most perilous seas, sinking the *Copenhagen* was going to be a tough pill for Anderson to swallow.

From a distance, the crew could see a twin rotor helicopter approaching from the east, heading in their direction. As it got it closer, they saw a cargo container visibly hanging from beneath the chopper, with a Nordic logo gleaming in the afternoon sun.

Anderson and his crew stared at the odd spectacle moving across the sky until it disappeared beyond the horizon. The container was cut loose, hitting the water with a large splash. The metal box floated for a few minutes before sinking to the bottom of the ocean.

Arriving at the preset coordinates about ten nautical miles west of Catalina Island, a call came over the *Copenhagen's* radio. "Captain Anderson, this is Admiral Jeff Paulson aboard the USS Stockdale on your starboard side. Sir, we need you to bring your engines to a full stop and prepare your crew for a roof extraction by helicopter. Please acknowledge."

"This is Captain Anderson. We are preparing the vessel as instructed and heading to the roof," Anderson quickly replied.

As the *Copenhagen's* engines and systems were being shut down, an orange and white SH-60 Coast Guard helicopter arrived and hovered just above the ship's bridge.

Anderson ordered his crew members up the ladder to the roof with lifejackets. One by one the crew were lifted into the hovering chopper by rescue basket as the flotilla of military vessels surrounding the ship began rapidly steaming away from the doomed ship.

With the *Copenhagen's* crew safely evacuated, a squadron of Navy F/18 Hornet fighter jets that had been circling the area in formation descended on the abandoned vessel, launching their harpoon anti-ship missiles. The harpoons skimmed just above the surface of the ocean at over 500mph before slamming into the hull of the massive container ship.

The explosions that rocked the ship could be seen and heard up and down the Southern California coast. What remained of the *Copenhagen* and its cargo sank rapidly into the ocean depths.

“Raven Rock, this is Angel Flight Leader—over.”

“This is Secretary Metcalf at Command Center, go ahead,” came the reply.

“Madame Secretary, be advised: the *Copenhagen* has been destroyed with no secondary nuclear detonations.”

“We see that on our video feed, Angel Leader. Well done,” Metcalf said, looking around at the satisfied and relieved faces inside Raven Rock.

“This is the President,” a firm voice suddenly sounded over the network. “We have the all-clear, and we’re heading back to the White House.”

As cheers echoed through the Raven Rock bunker, Jim and Laura held hands, trying as best they could to process the devastating news about Tom Fahey and the whirlwind of tumultuous events that had brought them so close together.

TRIAGE

CHAPTER 34

Mossad Headquarters, Tel Aviv Israel

News of Tom Fahey's betrayal spread quickly throughout the intelligence community, but none took it harder than the leadership team at Mossad headquarters in Tel-Aviv. Director Shai Cohen was visibly devastated by the news of his long-time friend and colleague. A betrayal of Fahey's proportion had not been seen since the British discovered their superstar agent Kim Philby was a Russian double agent.

In the business world, defections and betrayals impacted the bottom line. In the clandestine service, defection and betrayal put people's lives in jeopardy and forever tainted the reputations of innocent people. Guilt by association. This was Director Cohen's biggest fear—that his close personal relationship with a known double agent could be the kiss of death for his own career. To think that a lifetime of service to Israel and Mossad could be forever in question was too much for him to bear.

Cohen tried instead to focus on the mission at hand, which was to get to the bottom of the Al-Qaeda attack on America and Panama. He gathered his team to review the data and walk through the timeline of events to see where they might find clues.

"The Iranians have been clever," Cohen said to General Benjamin Green. "First, they secretly developed functional nuclear weapons against all standing international agreements and treaties, and then hid those weapons right under our noses. Next, they staged a robbery to make it look like we stole their weapons and then leaked it to the media so they could make us look like assholes. Does that about sum it up, General?"

"Yes, it does."

"We know all this is true, and so do the Americans, but we have no proof. The Iranians are banking on plausible deniability, and without any substantiated proof of their involvement, it will be difficult to take any military action."

"Director, we can extract Darzi out of Iran and interrogate him in a neutral location," the General said. "That little shit has to be involved in this, and we can get him to talk."

"Darzi would die before we got him to talk," Cohen said.

"What about just taking him out permanently?" the General offered. "He's been involved in enough activity against Israel to warrant a kill order."

"I agree, General. The problem is that killing Darzi doesn't prove Iran's complicity in the Al-Qaeda attack," Cohen shot back.

A voice suddenly came over Cohen's intercom. "Director, I have Pakistan Chief of Station Leah Hoffman on the line from Islamabad. She says it's urgent."

"Send her through Gina," Cohen replied.

"Director Cohen, good afternoon," Hoffman began.

"Leah, I have you on speaker phone with General Green and the rest of the leadership team. Please go ahead," Cohen said into the speaker.

"Director, we've just had a walk-in at our Embassy here in Islamabad." W*alk-in* was a term used to describe an agent who voluntarily walks into a foreign embassy and offers information. It was rare and highly unusual, especially at Israeli embassies.

"Did you say a walk-in?" Cohen clarified.

"Yes. He says his name is Aref Hashemi. Claims to be an Iranian nuclear engineer who was trained here in Pakistan."

There was a sudden barrage of typing as support staff in the Tel Aviv conference room started to research the name on their laptop databases.

"What does Hashemi want?" Cohen asked.

"Sir, he is asking for political asylum. He says he can tell us everything we want to know about Iran's role in supporting the Al-Qaeda terrorist attack on the U.S."

"Go on," Cohen said with more than a little apprehension.

"He claims to have been one of three scientists inside Iran's nuclear development program. He says he was involved in the development of the two nukes that were being hidden under Persepolis." As the conversation continued, support analysts in the conference room tapped loudly on their laptops to crossmatch data on known Iranian nuclear experts.

"Director, our current intelligence doesn't show anyone using this name being involved in Iran's nuclear program," Hoffman said.

"We didn't know Iran was able to actually build operational nukes, so it's not surprising that Hashemi's name is unknown," General Green interjected.

"Any dipshit watching the news right now could put together a story like this and try to sell it to an Embassy in return for asylum," Cohen countered.

"That's true, Director. But of all the embassies you could walk into with this information, why would someone choose to walk into our embassy?" the General asked. "This guy knows that if Israel gets solid proof of Iranian complicity in this thing, we will come down on Tehran militarily in the most aggressive way possible."

"So?"

"So, Mr. Hashemi must be really pissed off with someone in Tehran. He's giving us this information so we'll go in there and kick some ass," the General added.

"I agree with that assessment, Director," Hoffman replied. "The way this guy is talking, it sounds like his motivation is revenge," she added.

"Leah, we need rock-solid confirmation from your walk-in that Iran only built two nukes. We need incontrovertible proof that the robbery at Persepolis was staged and that Iran was complicit in the nuclear weapons transfer to Al-Qaeda. Proof, Leah. Do you believe this guy is telling you the truth?" Cohen asked directly.

"I do, Sir."

"And what makes you so confident in your assessment?"

"Sir, his right hand is missing just above the wrist. Not pretty. He says Darzi from Iran's Republican Guard chopped it off with a meat cleaver. No anesthesia."

"No wonder Mr. Hashemi is so pissed off," General Green muttered with a smirk.

"I believe the hand we confiscated at the scene under Persepolis will belong to Mr. Hashemi," Hoffman said.

As Cohen and his team processed the information coming in from Pakistan, it was generally agreed that the missing hand was enough for Hashemi to be considered a credible informant.

proof that the recovery of Persepolis was [illegible] here [illegible] an [illegible] was completed in the nuclear [illegible] to [illegible] Parrot Lane [illegible] not believe this crude telling of the [illegible] which had [illegible].

[illegible]

And what [illegible] in your losses at [illegible]

"Six [illegible] missing [illegible] the world. [illegible] says [illegible] from [illegible] and Republican [illegible] chopped [illegible] off with a [illegible]."

"No wonder Mr. Hashi [illegible] entered with [illegible]."

"I believe [illegible] were [illegible] at the [illegible] belonged to Mr. Ha [illegible]."

[illegible] and [illegible] procession [illegible] in [illegible] it was generally agreed [illegible] missing hand was [illegible] considered a [illegible].

TWO MONTHS LATER

CHAPTER 35

Tilanqiao Prison: Shanghai, China

Prisoners 43456 and 28905 sat quietly in their cells. They hadn't been allowed to shave or shower in more than two weeks, and their orange overalls were dark with grime and perspiration.

Four military guards in green uniforms and bright white gloves entered their cells, quickly applying handcuffs and leg shackles. The prisoners made eye contact outside their respective cells just before being escorted down the dimly lit hallway and outside into the large, rectangular prison yard.

The yard was a swath of orange clad inmates, standing against the prison's filthy gray walls. The condemned were shuffled into the center of the courtyard together, their ankle chains rattling around their feet. Guards held the prisoners' elbows and shoulders tightly, forcing them to stand at attention in front of Warden Tan.

The Warden opened a small brown envelope containing the official sentencing decree from China's Ministry of State Security and read it aloud for all the prisoners to hear.

"Premier Li Wan 43456 and Minster Gao Zheng 28905 have been found guilty of high treason by the Ministry of State Security and the People's Republic of China. They are hereby sentenced to death. By order of China's Minister of State Security, Jiang Peng, the sentence is to be carried out immediately."

The two inmates, half dazed, legs giving way beneath them, struggled to hear the Warden's proclamation as the execution process began. They were forced to kneel on the yard's cobblestones, pain shooting into their knees. Dirty washcloths from the prison's canteen were tied around the prisoner's faces, serving as makeshift blindfolds. The rags reeked of garbage just as Minister Jiang Peng and his father had intended. As they knelt, the two convicts helplessly soiled themselves.

The inmates in the yard looked on in silence as two tall executioners from Shanghai's army garrison walked over and stood behind the condemned. They drew their service revolvers, aiming them just inches from the prisoners' skulls. Two loud cracks rang out across the courtyard as the bullets fired into the prisoner's heads, their bodies tumbling awkwardly to the ground. Two streams of blood flowed together into a single pool around what remained of the inmates' skulls.

Looking on from the gallery, not a single prisoner fainted, gagged, or vomited.

Warden Tan collected the spent bullet casings and placed them in envelopes. The traitors' families in Beijing would receive the government's invoice for the cost of the bullets via China Post by the end of the week.

In the prison infirmary, organs were harvested from the two corpses. Beijing's elite in need of a liver, kidney, or heart were never fussy about who it came from. What remained of the prisoners' headless and gutted bodies was shoveled into the prison furnace.

Minister Jiang Peng's vision for a more legitimate and progressive China was beginning to take shape. The old guard would be purged by a new generation of leaders, just as his father had done many decades before. The bodies of Gao Zheng and Li Wan had been reduced to ashes, their names erased from the history books, never to be spoken of again.

REPRISALS

CHAPTER 36

CIA Headquarters: Langley, Virginia

Jim Keenan looked out the window of his new executive office and waited for the phone to ring.

"I have Beijing Chief Ken Barrow on line one, Sir."

"Put him through, please, Angela."

A firm male voice said, "Director Keenan, I want to offer my sincere congratulations on your promotion to CIA head honcho," Barrow began with a quip. "Seriously though Jim, the President couldn't have picked a better man to lead the Agency. And the youngest?"

"Then why do I feel a thousand years old? These last couple of months have been like drinking water from a firehouse."

"I bet," Barrow laughed.

"I have to say, Wentworth was gracious about stepping aside as Director, and he's been very helpful with the transition," Keenan offered.

"Jim, the President knew he had to clean up the CIA before the November election, and Wentworth knew he wasn't the right man for the job," Barrow added.

"I suppose that's true," Keenan replied, staring at the stacks of documents on his desk.

"And how is Laura handling her big promotion to FBI Deputy Director? You can bet old J. Edgar Hoover is rolling over in his grave," Barrow joked.

"Laura is one sharp cookie, Ken. She knew there was a bigger problem at CIA long before anyone else figured it out. She originally suspected Wentworth."

She wasn't far off," Barrow added. "And that's one of the things I need to talk to you about, Jim," Barrow said in a serious tone.

"Sure. What's happening in Beijing?"

"First of all, we can confirm that Premier Li and MSS Minister Gao Zheng were both executed at Tilanqiao Prison yesterday. The order was given by your friend, Jiang Peng. He's just been named the head of China's Ministry of State Security, and all our intelligence indicates he is slated to be the next President when his father retires."

"Peng is a guy we can work with, Ken. If we play our cards right, we could be looking at a whole new era of engagement between the U.S. and China. We can't try to crush them like we did the Soviet Union. We have to figure out a way to compete and coexist without killing each other. I know Jiang Peng believes the same thing. We need to take advantage of this opportunity."

"I understand."

There was a pause.

"There's something else, and I'm sorry to have to bring it up."

"Tom Fahey?" Keenan guessed.

"Yes. We can confirm that Fahey and his wife May Chiu are now here in Beijing. They turned up about three weeks ago. They've been given the full package. A big apartment, car, driver, generous pension. The works."

There was silence on the phone as Keenan processed the painful news. It wasn't unexpected, but it was still difficult to hear.

"Our internal investigation found that Beijing paid him millions of dollars over the last several years. All sent through his wife May Chiu's business accounts at the Bank of China. She purchased homes in Switzerland, Monte Carlo, and the Algarve in Portugal," Barrow said.

"We've been through it from top to bottom here as well, Ken. Turns out as the stock market was collapsing during the Al-Qaeda crisis, Tom was buying up stocks, in $500,000 increments."

"But why, Jim? What made him flip?"

"As best we can tell, his time working as an agent in Beijing had more of a profound impact on him than anyone realized. He became deeply entrenched with China's top political and business leaders, and they made him feel like royalty. They also made him very rich. He married the daughter of a PLA general who must have had some influence on his political views. He believed China could offer the world an alternative to western democracy. He clearly thought democracies were doomed. Too slow. Too ineffective. Bogged down by radical party politics."

"Do you think he knew about the Al-Qaeda plot?" Barrow asked.

"From what we can gather, Tom didn't know anything about the Al-Qaeda plot. When we discovered that China's MSS was withholding intelligence about the attacks, he was clearly taken by surprise and got really agitated. Looking back now, I could see a dramatic change in his demeanor."

"I have to take some responsibility for Fahey's escape, Jim. When I texted the contents of Jiang Peng's information to you and Wentworth at Raven Rock, I purposely left Fahey off the distribution, which I would never do normally. I think he figured it out. He must have known right then we were on to him."

"Don't punish yourself. If we hadn't flushed him out when we did, it could have gone on for years and cost a lot more lives. I need you to find the assets we have left in China under PROJECT LUCY and see what we can do for them. With Jiang Peng now heading MSS, we stand a very good chance of saving them instead of seeing them executed."

"We're already on it," Barrow said.

"When the time is right, I will contact Peng and see if we can quietly make a deal to extradite Tom back to the U.S. to stand trial for treason," Keenan replied. "We're going to be really busy over here at Langley for the next several months. Getting to the bottom of the terrorist attacks, crushing Iran with new sanctions, going after Al-Qaeda again in the Middle East, and of course, trying to rebuild Panama," Keenan said. "Please take care of China for us, Ken. We need you."

"I've got your back here, Jim," Barrow replied reassuringly. "Oh," he added as the call was about to end. "Congratulations!"

"You said that already," Keenan reminded him.

"No. I mean congratulations to you and Laura. America's new power couple."

"Thanks, Ken," he said with a chuckle. "It's hard to believe that something so wonderful could come out of something so horrific."

"A disaster is a terrible thing to waste," Barrow said, quoting someone he couldn't remember.

"Laura's changed me. I'm ready share my life with someone other than the Agency."

RENEWAL

CHAPTER 37

September 11: Midtown Manhattan

On a crisp, clear fall morning in Manhattan, the city's September 11th remembrance ceremonies around Ground Zero drew to a close. A long line of the fire department's bravest made their way up to Midtown and stood shoulder to shoulder along 8th Avenue. Their class A dress uniforms, white hats, and clean gloves shone in the bright autumn sunshine. Bagpipers from the FDNY's Emerald Society Pipe and Drum led a procession up the Avenue, playing *Scotland the Brave* as they marched in perfect unison, their green kilts, black feather bonnets, and white spats illuminated by the bright blue morning sky.

Engine 55 and Ladder 5 rolled slowly behind the marching Pipe and Drum, their red lights flashing with an occasional blast of the sirens to please the crowd. A four-member honor guard from the United States Naval

Academy marched several paces behind the firetrucks. Wearing their service dress whites, the Midshipmen carried the Stars and Stripes together with the U.S. Navy Flag, their colors waving gently in the soft autumn breeze.

At the end of the procession, a large white carriage and brown horse from Central Park trotted in time, hoofs clapping rhythmically against the pavement. Laura Bowman, dressed in a simple, white wedding dress and lace veil, held a bouquet of late summer flowers and waved to well-wishers who had gathered along the street. Laura's mother Kathleen sat next to her daughter as they made their way to the Midtown Firehouse.

"I can't think of a better maid of honor," Laura said to her mother. "You've helped so much. I don't know how you managed everything after Dad was killed. You must have been devastated."

"I held things together because of you," her mother answered. "But I couldn't have done it without the help of this FDNY family. They loved your father as much as I did. These men and women helped raise you after Dad died. You're one of them. That's why they want to make this day special for you, and to honor Battalion Chief Gregory Bowman."

"Everything is so beautiful," Laura exclaimed, looking around at the parade of colors.

"Your dad would have loved to hear those bagpipes. They always made his tough Scottish Highlander façade tear up," Kathleen Bowman said, her eyes growing misty.

"Jim is the love of my life, Mom. I've waited so long for a man who could love me and who I could love back. I was convinced that person didn't exist. It was like being hit by a lightning bolt the first time I met him. I just knew."

"Your dad always wanted the best for you, and I think you've found it."

Laura shot her mother a grin. "Dad's still watching out for us, Mom."

"This is the first September 11th anniversary where we can honor the memory of your father and his men, and at the same time, turn the day into something positive. Something we can finally celebrate," Kathleen Bowman said. "Let's make sure we enjoy it."

The procession and the carriage arrived at the front of the Battalion 8 Firehouse. Inside, Jim Keenan, dressed in a blue suit with a white shirt, light blue tie, and red carnation, stood in front of seated relatives and friends from both families. Hundreds of colorful flower bouquets adorned the interior of the fire station—a wedding gift from David Keenan's former colleagues at State Street Bank.

James stood with his mother Mary, waiting for the bride to enter.

"You know you could have chosen a real best man, Jimmy," Mary Keenan whispered to her son.

"Sometimes, Mom, the best man for the job is a woman," he quipped. "You were my very first best friend, and I can't think of anyone I would rather have next to me today."

"Your father would be proud of you, Jimmy," Mary sighed, poised between a sad memory and a joyful celebration.

"I miss him every day, Mom."

"I do too."

Surrounded by family and a large contingent of the New York City Fire Department, Laura Marie Bowman and James Francis Keenan exchanged vows and were married. It was a momentous time of celebration for two people whose lives had been forged by the events of 9-11, and a welcome time of renewal for a courageous firehouse in Midtown Manhattan that had given its last full measure of devotion on that tragic day, so many years ago.

EPILOGUE

In the post 9-11 era, America had slowly grown complacent, as deadly terrorist networks in the Middle East renewed their Jihad against the West, and China rapidly expanded its influence around the globe.

The attacks on Los Angeles and Panama were a blunt reminder that the world remained a dangerous place, and that America remained vulnerable. It also highlighted the precarious relationship between the United States and China, and the need to develop a more comprehensive level of engagement in the future.

On his first anniversary as CIA Director, Jim Keenan wrote an essay for the Council on Foreign Relations outlining the role of leadership in securing a new world order:

"The future of global economic and geopolitical stability will depend on the United States and its relationship with China, and this will require a new breed of political leadership on both sides of the Pacific. Leaders who are willing to embrace the cultural and political differences between East and West while at the same time working to find areas of common ground and mutual cooperation.

The United States will need to heighten its efforts as the standard bearer for fair trade, the rule of law, and human rights, and be willing to project strength in defending freedom and democracy wherever those values may be in jeopardy. For its part, China must be willing to finally stand on its own two feet and become an active participant in world events, rather than just an opportunistic observer.

The fate of the free world will ultimately depend on a new generation of leaders willing to engage and find solutions despite political and ideological differences. It will call for intelligent leaders who take the time to understand the lessons of history, and above all, courageous leaders who will, in the most difficult of circumstances, *Dare to be True.*"

JFK, Langley Virginia

ABOUT THE AUTHOR

Peter Levesque is an international supply chain expert and author, with more than thirty years of experience living and working in the Asia Pacific Region. He is the past Chairman of the American Chamber of Commerce in Hong Kong and serves on the Board of the U.S. Chamber of Commerce in Washington D.C. Levesque is the author of *The Shipping Point*, *The Rise of China*, and the *Future of Retail Supply Chain Management*, and has been featured on CNBC, BBC, Bloomberg, The New York Times, and The Wall Street Journal. He resides in South Florida and Cape Cod, Massachusetts with his wife Lisa and their three children.

Printed in the USA
CPSIA information can be obtained
at www.ICGtesting.com
LVHW091557110724
785247LV00025B/204/J

9 798986 320199